THE ARMY RANGER'S SURPRISE

the Men of
At-Ease Ranch

D1714333

THE ARMY RANGER'S SURPRISE

the Men of
At-Ease Ranch

DONNA MICHAELS

Entangled Publishing, LLC
2614 South Timberline Road
Suite 105, PMB 159
Fort Collins, CO 80525
rights@entangledpublishing.com

Lovestruck is an imprint of Entangled Publishing, LLC.

Edited by Heather Howland
Cover design by Heather Howland
Cover photography by PeopleImages/Getty Images

Manufactured in the United States of America

First Edition July 2018

Once again, I'd like to dedicate this book to all the readers who asked for Vince's and Leo's stories. This was a very special "write" for me.

And to those whose lives have been touched by suicide in any way. You have my heart and my support.

Chapter One

Restlessness was a bitch.

Until recently, Leo Reed had been perfectly content to spend his free time on At-Ease, the ranch his Army Ranger buddies opened to help veterans transition back into society. *He* was one of those vets. Hell, he was the reason *behind* the ranch, thanks to relentless pain, too much booze, and too damn many memories in his head that led to poor judgment and two hospitalizations he wasn't proud of.

All of that was in his past. The carnage-heavy memories that used to taunt him with images of those he failed to save no longer ate at him day in, day out. He could start to move on—live again—but not if he clung to the ranch. Lately, he itched to do more. See more. Be more.

But more what?

Leo finished his shower, got dressed, then sat on his bed and shoved his feet into his boots.

Although he could relate to some of the sullen veterans staying in several of the bunkhouses and who had just sat in the group therapy session that finished downstairs, the suffocating dark cloud that used to follow and surround him no longer existed. Seeking help, both here at the ranch and at the rec center near his grandmother, plus the support of family and friends had motivated him to crawl out of the pit and back into society.

Trouble was he wasn't sure what to do. Or with whom. All his buddies were in relationships. He lived with two of them and their significant others.

Grabbing his packed duffel bag, he headed downstairs in the main house they all shared.

"Hey, Leo." Stone came out of the kitchen carrying tortilla chips and salsa. "You're just in time for movie night. Vince is making popcorn, and Jovy and Emma are in the rec room grabbing the drinks."

Jovy was Stone's wife, and Emma was Vince's fiancée. Over the past fifteen months, all four of Leo's Ranger buddies had fallen in love. Two were married, and the other two were engaged. He was the lone bachelor of the Ranger Rifle Unit.

Stone frowned. "Do you remember whose turn it is to pick the movie?"

"It's the girls' turn," Vince replied, exiting the kitchen with two big bowls of popcorn that filled the room with a buttery aroma that made Leo's mouth water.

Hah. Any chance the guys had of watching car chases and gunfights just went out the window. Leo had shared enough Friday night movie nights to know the women usually chose a romantic comedy.

Stone motioned with his head to the duffel bag in Leo's hand. "Where are you off to?"

"I'm heading to my grandmother's for the weekend." He slung the strap over his shoulder, never more grateful to have a legitimate reason to leave. Watching a chick flick while the couples snuggled on the couch was getting old. Not that he wasn't happy for his friends. He was, but it was damned awkward, and a reminder of all that he lacked. Like a clean past worthy of getting involved with someone. Courting a girl was out of the question.

Helping his mom out, however, was a different story. She was in Galveston, assisting his sister who just had twins, and he knew it would ease her mind if he checked in on his grandmother a little more often while she was away.

It would also ease *his* mind. Ava Pendleton was a senior citizen who acted like a feisty thirty-year-old. Without his mom around to keep his gram out of trouble, he decided to stay on the weekends and check in on her once throughout the week, too.

"That's too bad," Stone said. "The girls will be disappointed, because they picked the movie just for you."

He lifted his brows. "They did? Which one?"

"*Captain America: The Winter Soldier.*" Vince grinned.

Leo grimaced. Christ, if he had a nickel for every time someone told him he looked like the actor who played the Winter Soldier, he'd have enough money to finance a damn movie.

Stone chuckled. "I thought you'd approve."

Leo flipped him off.

The asshole chuckled louder, and Vince joined in. Now they were both on his shit list. He would've told them, too, but they glanced at the girls in the other room and got sappy looks on their faces.

That strange restlessness whispered through Leo again. It occurred more and more whenever he was around the couples. Witnessing devotion soften their expressions made him feel an emotion he'd never felt before. Envy.

Time to go.

He adjusted the strap on his shoulder and cleared his throat. "Enjoy your movie."

"You need to get yourself a woman and bring her here for

movie night," Stone told him.

An image of a pretty brunette drifted through Leo's mind with perfect clarity, thanks to his photographic memory.

Kaydee. His grandmother's neighbor. With a ready smile, infectious laughter, and a warm brown gaze that mesmerized and drew him in, she was half the reason he was eager to spend the weekend up there.

More than half. Although he'd never tell her.

He couldn't head down that road. In order to achieve the kind of a relationship his buddies had with their women, he'd have to open up and share his past and all the damn shame and guilt that came with it. No woman deserved that.

No woman deserved the mess that was *him*.

Better to leave things alone and settle for the enjoyment he got from living on the ranch and working at Foxtrot, the construction company his buddies owned.

"You could always bring her here for a nice picnic. I can whip up something simple for you to eat," Vince said. "And you know Emma would be happy to bake you a pie."

And he'd be happy to leave the damn conversation. "Thanks, but it's not necessary. Have a great weekend."

Without waiting for their reply, he pivoted on his heel and walked out the door. Taking it upon himself to spend more time with his grandmother wasn't just a great reason to leave the ranch, it was also a great reason to possibly bump into Kaydee. She lived across the street and a few houses down from his grandmother. He should know—he'd helped her move in to one side of the duplex and her grandfather move in to the other last September.

He got in his truck and started the hour's drive north toward Dallas with the woman on his mind. Being around her always brought a sense of calm. She looked at him through these gorgeous brown eyes that conveyed a warmth he felt right down to his boots. And her upbeat, sunny disposition—

which he normally shied away from—always made him feel alive. It was almost addicting. Hell, it *was* addicting, and lately, he found himself going through withdrawal.

Not long after she moved in, he started to run into her at the rec center, mostly on senior citizen night when he was there to pick his grandmother up from bingo. Not that his spirited grandmother wasn't capable of driving. No. She could drive, just not without a license. Too many speeding tickets saw to that. Yeah, his gram had a bit of a lead foot. But he was grateful for it, because he sometimes got to meet Kaydee at the center when she was there to get her grandfather.

You need to get yourself a woman.

Stone's words echoed through Leo's mind. If he were to follow that advice, then Kaydee was the one he'd pursue. His pulse kicked up a notch at the thought, then slowed to a crawl. The point was moot. A woman as bright and shiny as Kaydee deserved better than him and his dark past.

By the time he pulled into Gram's driveway and cut the engine, he'd put those foolish thoughts aside. No sense in entertaining something so far out of reach. He wasn't the type to live with his head in the clouds. More like stuck in the dirt.

With a snicker rumbling up his throat, he knocked twice before entering. It was his normal ritual, and he enjoyed hearing his grandmother huff that he should just walk in without knocking. Today, she didn't pay him any mind.

No. She was too damn busy sitting on the couch necking with the neighbor.

What the hell?

Leo made the mistake of sucking in a breath while still snickering. Now he coughed and sputtered, which broke the couple apart.

His grandmother arched a brow. "What? I'm eighty-one. Not dead."

And he was never going to get that damn image out of his head.

"You're late. We ate without you." Her voice was stern, but her gaze twinkled. "I saved you a plate. It's on the kitchen counter."

"Thanks." He transferred his gaze to the man she just checked for tonsils. "Nate."

With the same twinkle in his eyes and *I'm not sorry* expression as his grandmother, the guy smiled. "Good to see you, Leo."

Gram waved toward the kitchen. "Go on. Eat your supper while I continue to have my dessert."

His stomach rolled. Twice. Fuck. Eating wasn't an option now. But standing there was even worse. Christ, he didn't need more images of his gram going at it hot and heavy in his head. Fighting his gag reflex, he scrambled from the room, booked it through the dining room and straight into the kitchen…and stopped dead.

Kaydee stood by the sink with her back to him while she washed dishes. Except she wasn't exactly standing. She had a set of white earbuds in her ears and was either dancing or doing some kind of ritual for the dishwashing gods.

Intrigued, Leo dropped his duffel in the corner and leaned against the wall to watch the show. A smile twitched his lips. Her moves were uncoordinated, but her enthusiasm was stellar. The woman gave everything her all. Dancing… badly. Caring for her grandfather by giving up her own place to move next to him. Her garden, which bordered both sides of her house in a mixture of flowers and vegetables—because she'd gotten the seeds mixed up.

Kaydee's ability to embrace her mistakes and turn them into something positive left him in awe.

So did the way her jeans hugged her sweet ass. They conformed to her rounded curves like a second skin, and the more she moved the more his zipper bit into his thickening erection. Not good. Guilt propelled him forward to put an end to his viewing pleasure.

As he neared, he cleared his throat a few times, but she didn't hear him, just continued to dance and test both his integrity and that of his zipper. Damn thing wasn't the only object ready to burst. His whole groin was hard and throbbing now. A reaction he'd grown accustomed to around her.

"Kaydee," he said as she wiggled while spraying a pot with water.

Bubbles formed and overflowed, much like the awareness rushing through his body. She had him harder than the damn pot. His attraction to the woman intrigued him as much as it scared the hell out of him.

"*Kaydee,*" he said again, but this time he reached out to lightly touch her shoulder.

Letting out a startled cry, she turned toward him with the sprayer still in her hand. Water immediately pelted his face and the side of his head with the force of a mini power washer, blasting his flesh with a shock of heat that ran down his neck and chest. Luckily, it was only hot and not scalding.

"Oh my God, Leo!" She dropped the sprayer, then shut off the water with one hand and yanked her earbuds out with the other. "Are you okay?

"Yeah. I needed a good soaking." He slicked back his wet hair and grinned. "No harm done."

But apparently, she chose not to listen, because she grabbed a nearby dish towel and started to mop the wetness from his face and chest. "I'm so sorry. I didn't hear you come in."

"I know."

She stilled, and her gaze slowly rose to meet his. "Oh, crap. Exactly how long were you in here?"

Loving the flush of color that swept up into her cheeks,

he decided to tease her a little more. "Long enough to know you'd be dangerous on the dance floor."

"Yeah, to others." Her blush increased. "Oh God, I can't believe you saw that."

Before he could reply, she dropped her forehead on his chest, and her whole body shook as she laughed.

The unexpected move and feel of her soft curves brushing his body removed all traces of teasing from his mind. He always wondered how she'd feel in his arms, and now he knew, even if—technically—he didn't have his arms around her. Yet. Because he could. It'd be so easy. So damn easy. All he had to do was put his hands on her back.

But that would be playing with fire, and he didn't want her to get burned.

"I can't believe I got you soaking wet." She drew back and started mopping his shirt with the towel again. "I'm so sorry."

Thankful for the reprieve, he went back to teasing. "No harm done. I won't melt."

She snickered and continued to dry him off, but her nearness and press of her fingers weren't doing his libido any good, so he placed his hand over hers to stop her movements.

Big mistake.

Before, at least a wet shirt had separated their skin. Not now. His palm covered her hand, and the feel of her soft, warm skin kicked his pulse into gear.

Once again, their gazes met, but this time mortification and teasing were no longer present, just a raw, untamed attraction. It posed a danger big enough to rival her lethal dance moves.

Her gaze dropped to his mouth, and Leo's heart rocked in his chest. A sensation he hadn't felt in years. Leave it to Kaydee to induce the movement. It was strange. He knew he should back away, but he didn't. Couldn't. It felt as if his whole body was coming alive, and until that moment, he hadn't realized how truly out of touch with life he'd been the past few years. Perhaps always.

Would he wake up even more if they kissed?

Ignoring the red flags going off in his head, he lifted his other hand to cup her chin and slowly lowered his mouth.

"Is everything all right?" his gram called out from the other room. "I thought I heard Kaydee scream."

The startled woman in his arms jumped back and turned to face the sink. "Everything's fine. I just didn't hear Leo come in, that's all," she called over her shoulder before returning her attention to the dishes. Too bad she didn't save some for the sprayer, because she fumbled with it, and this time, she managed to get herself wet. "Dammit."

Leo handed her the towel, but kept his mouth shut. Mostly because he was trying to keep from laughing.

"Thanks." She mopped up her shirt and glanced at him. "Shut up. Not a word."

Then she burst out laughing.

He joined her. It'd been a long time since he'd laughed with pure abandon. It felt good. Kaydee always made him feel good, and he was finding it harder and harder to fight his attraction to her.

It was a sobering thought. He didn't want to be attracted to her or anyone. And yet he was, and he was beginning to realize he had no damn control over it.

• • •

Kaydee Wagner was laughing on the outside, but on the inside she was trying very hard not to give in to the urge to snuggle against her hot friend. Again. It hadn't been her intention earlier, but when she'd stupidly drenched the poor guy with hot water she'd forgotten to keep her distance. Just thinking about it now sent another wave of heat into her face, and it burned as she recalled how her embarrassment had turned to bliss. When she'd set her head against Leo's wet chest, she couldn't stop from melting into his incredible, hard, sexy body.

A treat for sure. She'd always had sort of a secret thing for Sebastian Stan in the Marvel movies, but Sebastian had nothing on Leo Reed. The handsome former Army Ranger had starred in her fantasies ever since they met. But he was so out of her league. Guys like him only wanted to be friends with girls like her. A fact he'd proven several times over the past few months, even though she'd caught him looking at her with interest in his gorgeous blue eyes.

That was okay, though. Thanks to growing up an army brat, Kaydee had learned early in life how to adjust and move on. She was far from good girlfriend material anyway. Thanks to that army brat lifestyle, "restlessness" was her middle name. She never stayed in one place more than two or three years. Putting down roots was not in her wheelhouse.

Besides, she didn't have a lot of free time, between her long list of household repairs, part-time job at the salon, and helping her friend find a location to open a beauty shop. Yeah, she was too preoccupied to date.

Still, there was something about this man that made her want to hug him and never let go. It was a new and peculiar feeling.

The moment Leo had appeared from out of the blue in her yard and offered to help when she and her grandfather had been struggling to carry a couch into her grandfather's side of the house, Kaydee was smitten. She knew right then that he was different. Between his generosity, good manners, gorgeous blue eyes, and panty-melting smile, she was never the same.

"Want some help with the dishes?" he asked, bringing

her mind back to the present.

See? Most men would've made fun of her startled reaction, scarfed down their food, then handed her their dirty dish.

Not Leo.

"No. You eat." She motioned toward his covered dish on the counter. "Thank God your food withstood my water attack."

For months now, she had enjoyed his company both here at his grandmother Ava's and at the rec center. Each encounter left her wanting more and looking forward to the next one. This was way out of character for someone who never got attached to people outside of family. Except for her friend from work and Ava. But Ava was their neighbor, and since her grandfather was probably going to stay at his current address for the rest of his life, she reasoned it was okay to befriend the woman.

Who was she kidding? Ava was a hoot. She was sassy and shot straight from the hip. Qualities Kaydee admired. As for the woman's grandson, she admired his sense of family and how he helped people, whether it was support for other veterans or lending a hand and backbone to an old man and his granddaughter on moving day.

And she really liked the bad-boy look he had going on.

His hair was dark and wavy, and she knew it hadn't been cut in a few years. The itch to style it was strong, but the look actually worked for Leo. Really well. As did the delicious five-o'clock shadow covering his strong jaw. She bet it would feel amazing against her skin. And his eyes...damn, they were a startling blue that could switch from a hardened I-don't-give-a-damn expression to wicked amusement with a mere blink.

Kind of like the way he regarded her now.

He smiled. "Unlike our shirts."

What were they talking about again? She glanced at

what was in his hands. Oh. Right. His food not being ruined. "Yeah." She snorted. "I'm going to have to go home and change before I head to the rec center."

"Rec center?" He stuck his plate in the microwave. "Is there something going on tonight for seniors?"

"No." She finished rinsing the last dish. "I need to hang up some flyers." A thrill rippled through her. "My idea got approved."

Last month, on behalf of herself and her coworker, Fiona, she'd petitioned the board of directors from the nonprofit corporation that ran the center to hold a "cutting clinic" once a month to offer free haircuts to senior citizens, veterans, and the disabled. But truthfully, she and Fiona wouldn't turn anyone away. And the proceeds from any donations would go to a different charity each month.

"That's terrific. Congratulations!" He pulled her in for a quick hug, then released her just as quickly. "I knew they'd go for it. When do you start?"

Her body was still tingling from contact with his solid muscles, and it took a moment to get her mind back on track. "Next month. We'll hold the clinic the first Tuesday of every month, from six to eight p.m."

"This will be a great way for you to drum up some word-of-mouth business for Fiona's future shop."

He was aware that she worked with Fiona, and that her friend wanted to strike out on her own. What he didn't know—what no one knew—was that Fiona repeatedly asked Kaydee to partner in the venture, and she always declined. Owning a business was a root, and restless spirits didn't have roots. Not that she ever planned her moves. They were always triggered by an overwhelming suffocating feeling that hit her like a bug and spurred her to move on. She'd just let people down if she tied herself to a business or person. Without attachments, it was much easier to pick up and leave when the urge hit...and the urge would hit.

It always did.

The microwave beeped. "Any luck finding a location?" he asked, retrieving his plate.

For the past two months, she'd helped her friend work on a business plan, and they recently started to search for a place for Fiona to lease.

"Not so far." The spaces were either too run-down, in a bad part of town, or way out of Fiona's financial reach. But neither of them were a quitter. They'd find something. Sooner or later opportunity would show itself; she was sure of it. Mostly.

"Just remember what I told you about my friends. They own property in Joyful and would be willing to work out a good deal for Fiona to lease one of their shops."

Her heart warmed as it had last month when he first made the suggestion. "Thank you. And I promise, she's keeping it in mind. It's just that an hour is a little too far for some of her regulars to travel, and she's counting on them to follow her to her shop."

"And the new customers she's going to pick up from the rec center," he said.

She nodded. "True. I'm so grateful you encouraged me to submit that proposal to the board."

"That success was all yours, Kaydee." He tugged the silverware drawer open and grabbed a fork. "I had nothing to do with it."

Every time she tried to pay the darn guy a compliment, he rebuffed it. Not this time. "There wouldn't *be* any success if you hadn't suggested writing the proposal in the first place."

She hadn't had a clue where to start. Leo was the one who pointed her in the right direction.

"Still—"

"Stop right there." She cut him off and gently shoved him

toward the table. "Take the thanks and go eat your food."

He blinked at her for a second before amusement replaced his somber expression. "Yes, ma'am." He saluted her with his free hand. "Geez, you take a step toward independence and you're suddenly giving orders."

"That's right. You got a problem with that?" Kaydee tried to hold a straight face, but amusement twitched her lips.

"Not at all." A slow, sexy grin spread across his face. "I've got no problem letting a woman in the driver's seat."

Awareness zinged through Kaydee's body, flooding her belly with a boatload of heat. If she hadn't been sure before, she was sure now. Leo was flirting with her.

Too bad she sucked at flirting. Still, she couldn't let the opportunity pass without trying. With warmth filling her cheeks, she forced herself to hold his devilish gaze and said the first thing that came to her befuddled mind. "Good to know."

He must've approved, because he gave her a winking nod.

Her pulse hiccuped. She had no idea how to respond to that, so she didn't. Instead, Kaydee pointed to his plate, and water dripped on the floor from her still-wet hand. "You really should eat before it gets cold again."

As she grabbed a paper towel and bent to wipe the floor, a thought occurred.

Was *she* the reason he hadn't scarfed down his food and left yet?

Nah. Couldn't be.

But when Kaydee straightened, she caught Leo checking out her butt. She drew in a breath. "Are you in here killing time on purpose?"

The sound of laughter and giggles drifted in from the other room.

Leo sat down at the table and winced. "Yeah, because

of that." He motioned toward the living room with his fork. "How long has that been going on?"

Disappointment squeezed Kaydee's chest. She should've known there was a purpose behind his open attention, and it had nothing to do with her. He was spending extra time with her to avoid the couple in the other room.

And that was the other reason for the invisible weight pressing down on her. For months, Ava and her grandfather had been flirting. It was about time they stopped circling each other. Kaydee thought it was cute how they held hands and carried on like teenagers. She also thought Leo would be happy for them. It really sucked to be wrong about that.

"This week," she finally replied. "Why? Don't you want them to be happy?"

"Yeah, of course. Trust me, I have no problem with them dating." He met her gaze, and the amusement-tinged honesty in his blue eyes soothed some of her disquiet. "I just don't want to walk in on them again when they're...*overjoying* in each other."

So she hadn't been wrong about him. But then the rest of the poor guy's words sank in, and Kaydee's eyes went wide. "Oh my God. You walked in on them...uh...making out?" She bit her lip, but it didn't stop her grin.

"Yes." A grimace rippled across his face. "That image will haunt me the rest of my life."

She laughed. "Then maybe you need a new image to focus on."

Dammit. That slipped out without permission.

Leo stilled for a full second before he turned toward her with a sexy, lopsided grin on his face. "Exactly what image do you have in mind, Kaydee?"

A fluttering instantly commenced in her belly. She couldn't tell if he was just toying with her or serious. Whatever it was, she was too befuddled to say something catchy. "It's a surprise," she said, unwilling to show fear. Or stupidity. She'd shown him enough of that tonight.

But apparently, she said something wrong, because the light disappeared from his gaze.

"I don't like surprises," he muttered, and turned his attention back to his food.

Her giddiness dimmed. Why didn't he like surprises? Did it have to do with his past?

Leo wasn't aware that she knew about what he'd gone through, and she wasn't about to bring it up. The guy had worked hard to overcome his demons and move on. He deserved happiness. Deserved to smile. Deserved some carefree moments in his life. And *carefree* happened to be something Kaydee was good at.

Now *that* was in her wheelhouse.

So she vowed, then and there, to show Leo that surprises could also be fun.

Chapter Two

Monday morning, Leo was back at the ranch, helping Stone and Vince install a drip edge and an ice and water shield to Vince and Emma's roof before they could lay down the roofing felt and shingles. He knew he needed to concentrate on the task at hand—the forecast called for rain later—but his mind kept drifting to Kaydee.

After they'd changed out of their wet clothes Friday night, he drove her to the rec center and throughout the local area to hang flyers. Not that she wasn't capable of handling the chore. He'd just been reluctant to part company with the upbeat woman, even after he'd gone and made everything uncomfortable with the "surprises" thing. Maybe even because of it, which was stupid on his part. Seeing her sunshine dim for even a second, being the cause of that flicker, made him want to kick his own ass.

And yet he'd stuck around. Her attitude was contagious. Leo felt lighter, happier...alive around Kaydee. Hell, even the act of breathing was easier. The invisible weight that had always compressed his shoulders and chest mysteriously lifted in her presence. Hanging out with her was a *positive*, and God knew positives had been missing from his life for far too long.

He just needed to try a hell of a lot harder to keep his shit contained. He never wanted to cast a shadow over her happiness like that again.

His apparent inability to tear himself away from Kaydee aside, he really didn't have anywhere else to go. He'd just left the ranch where he'd been a fifth wheel to a pair of amorous couples. He certainly hadn't wanted to be that at his grandmother's. In his darker days, he'd have gone to the bar, but that was a hell-fucking-no now. So it was either hole up in his room, intrude on Gram's privacy in the living room, or help the pretty neighbor.

No-brainer. Pretty neighbor would win every time.

"What do you think put that smile on his face?"

"Has to be his grandmother's pie."

"Yeah. You're right. I wonder what kind."

Stone and Vince's banter brought Leo's mind back to the present. He smirked. His grandmother actually *had* made him a pie yesterday. Of course, that wasn't the reason behind his smile, but those idiots didn't need to know.

He finished applying the last of the ice and water shield around the chimney, then glanced at Stone. "Blueberry."

A strangled sound rumbled in his buddy's throat. "Did you bring any back?"

Leo's lips twitched again. "No reason to. You don't need her pies when you have Emma living here."

"True." Stone nodded before sending Vince a stern look. "But it's fruitless when her fiancé scarfs most of it down without sharing."

Vince placed a roll of roofing felt down, then frowned at Stone. "I saved you a piece the last time."

"You left me a sliver that couldn't even fill a damn cavity,"

Stone grumbled.

Leo laughed. "You're as bad as Dom."

When he'd visited Dom last summer to check on Vince, who'd been there to help his brother convalesce after he was injured on active duty, Leo witnessed the pie-whore in action. He also noticed a change in Vince. For the better. Although his buddy was always ready with a smile, this was different. It was as if a switch had been flipped. Vince was happy. Content. And it was all due to his brother's neighbor, Emma.

Maybe there was something to caring for family members and meeting their neighbors.

"I wasn't a pie-whore until Emma started baking them."

Vince sat next to the roll and smiled, adoration filling his gaze. "Yeah, she's great. Isn't it funny how I'm the ranch cook, and my fiancée is a brilliant baker? And Stone runs At-Ease and the construction company, and his wife happens to be a brilliant businesswoman?"

Leo snorted. "And Cord is a stubborn Irishman, and Haley puts the *T* in tenacious."

Vince and Stone laughed as they rolled out the felt underlay.

When they were active-duty Army Rangers, they hadn't given Cord the nickname "Warlock" for nothing. The guy was a force to be reckoned with, able to see through even the thickest bullshit, but he'd met his match in his wife. They shared the same disposition and lack of patience, and it spilled into their relationship. Cord and Haley got engaged New Year's Day, and since they both wanted a quick and quiet wedding, they were married two weeks later.

"And my brother is…" Stone paused and narrowed his gaze. "What is Brick?"

Leo raised a brow. "A pain in the ass?"

"A giant?" Vince grinned.

"A giant pain in the ass," they said in unison before

laughing again.

The other Mitchum brother was an easygoing jokester, but he always had your back.

Stone snickered as he continued to apply the roofing felt. "Brick is a bull with a strong backbone and a sense of humor that sometimes gets in his way."

"Beth can be tough, too," Leo said. "And she has the patience of a saint."

Both good qualities for being Brick's fiancée.

"She needs it to deal with my brother." Stone laughed. "And how could she not have an abundance of patience? Poor woman grew up with Cord for a brother."

"True." Vince grinned at him. "Makes me wonder what your woman will do for a living, Leo."

His stomach knotted. With his past, she'd probably be a nurse. He pushed the dark thoughts aside and rolled out the next section. "I'm not in the market, so I guess it doesn't matter."

But the clear image of Kaydee's twinkling brown eyes and wide smile flashed through his head. He allowed his mind to consider her in the context of their discussion. She worked on people's hair, and he worked on people's houses. Not exactly a stellar connection like the others.

"Too bad, because Jovy's friend from Philly is flying in on Wednesday, and she's not only single, she's a pretty, petite blonde."

"Not interested," he said automatically. He preferred brunettes. Before he could stop it, that warm smile and those friendly brown eyes flashed through his mind again. "Besides, I'm checking on my grandmother after work on Wednesday." Maybe even see Kaydee.

A surge of warmth spread through his chest at the thought. Could he ask Kaydee out? Take a chance like his buddies? Each of them had, and now they were all living happy and content lives with women who cared about and supported them.

Then his past mistakes flashed through his mind, and the guilt that followed quickly chilled the warmth from his body.

Kaydee was too good for him. He had a history of letting people down. Even though he'd worked hard to rise above his past, he was still damaged goods, and she was kind and generous with a pure sweetness he wouldn't dare dilute.

Besides, if things went south—and they usually did for him—he'd ruin things between his grandmother and Kaydee. Put an unintentional strain on their friendship. And since his gram was *dating* Kaydee's grandfather, it was all the more reason to keep things platonic.

"Speaking of your grandmother, how's she doing without your mom around?" Vince asked.

Leo snorted, then went on to describe the scene he'd walked into last Friday.

"Holy shit, she's a character." Stone chuckled. "I hope we're that feisty when we reach her age."

"Hey, I'm like that now," Vince said with a grin.

Leo chuckled. "Tell me about it.

"Yeah," Stone said. "It's a good thing you're getting your own place soon."

Vince flipped their buddy off.

Stone snickered. "I'm just saying the walls aren't too thick in the main house."

"Or the floors." Vince smirked. "Your room's above ours."

A smile tugged Leo's lips. He was never more thankful his room was nowhere near either of theirs.

Vince started on another row. "Still, I have to admit, I can't wait for this house to be finished so Emma and I will have our own home on the ranch, like Brick and Beth."

It was then Leo realized that once Vince and Emma

moved, he would be the only one left out of the original five still in the house with Stone and Jovy. An invisible weight hit his shoulders and added to the heaviness already there. He was going to feel like a third wheel.

To hell with that.

"I should think about moving out, too," he said. "Is that apartment you own in town vacant?"

It was almost two years ago that he'd helped renovate the one-bedroom apartment above what was now a small café. Paying his way would make him feel better. He harbored enough guilt to last two lifetimes over what he'd put his friends and his family through.

"What?" Stone frowned. "No. I leased it out last month. Why do you want to move? You belong on this ranch. Aren't you happy here?"

"Yes. You know I am. That's not the point."

"Stone's right," Vince said. "You're as much a part of At-Ease as the rest of us."

"Damn straight. Once we're done with this house, we can start on yours."

Leo scowled. "No way."

They helped him enough. Too much. He hated mooching. Room and board were part of his salary at Foxtrot Construction, but that did not include them wasting time and money on him by building a house.

"Why the hell not?" A deep frown marred Stone's brow. "Brick has one, and we're working on Vince's now, so why don't you want a house on the ranch?"

"Because I don't deserve it."

"Bullshit." A rare spark of anger flashed in Vince's eyes. "Get thoughts like that out of your head right now."

Stone's face darkened. "Yeah. You have as much a right to live on this ranch as the rest of us."

He muttered a curse. "That's where you're wrong. Don't

you see? *You* all have the right, but I don't. I'm not part owner of this place. Just the reason for it. I just live and work here."

Vince and Stone stared at him with shock dropping their jaws. He was damn tired of being a burden. Hell, last year, he almost cost Stone his relationship with Jovy before he finally sought help. Having them build him a house wasn't fair. Hell no. It didn't sit well with him at all.

"Look, Stone. Thanks." He blew out a breath and held his friend's gaze. "I really do appreciate the offer, but it's not right. You've all sacrificed and invested so much in this ranch. Not me. I don't want special treatment. So, again, thanks, but I'm going to pass." He stood and motioned toward the graying sky. "Let's worry about getting this roof on before it rains."

Pivoting, he walked over to grab another roll of roofing felt and started on the other side, putting distance between them and an end to the conversation.

• • •

Two days later, Kaydee waited while her last client of the day moved from sitting under the dryer to the chair at her workstation.

"Work your magic, darling." Mrs. Hamilton's smiling gaze met hers in the mirror. "I have two barbecues this weekend."

"You got it." She returned her grin, then initiated the accustomed small talk while she removed the rollers and started to tease each section. Mrs. Hamilton loved big hair. *The bigger the better* was the sixty-three-year-old's motto. She was one of Kaydee's regulars at Yellow Rose Salon.

A twinge of guilt rippled through her chest. Both she and Fiona felt bad about the possibility of Fi taking clients away from their kind, elderly boss, but Rose would be the first to tell them it was a natural part of business. Business wasn't slow, and yet over the past few months, Rose had changed the shop hours. Yellow Rose Salon was now closed on weekends and shut down earlier a few nights during the week. Because of this, everyone's hours were cut. The change didn't hurt Kaydee too much, but it had spurred Fiona to pursue her dream of owning her own salon.

Silently contemplating the reason behind the altered hours, Kaydee worked on the last section of hair. She worried not only for Rose, but her boss's husband, too. He'd just retired from the postal service. The kind couple deserved to enjoy his retirement without health issues.

"You are a master," Mrs. Hamilton gushed, admiring herself in the mirror when Kaydee finished. "Perfect! Now, just hair-spray the hell out of it so it doesn't move an inch."

"Yes, ma'am." Smiling, Kaydee picked up the can and sprayed away. Not even wind would get through those locks.

After a satisfied Mrs. Hamilton left, Kaydee was still writing the woman's next appointment in the book when Fiona arrived a little early for her shift. Most days, they shared one, but today her friend needed the closing shift in order to take her visiting mother to the airport that morning.

It was the month for visiting mothers. Leo's mom was visiting her daughter, too. Which brought the handsome man into her neighborhood a little more often than normal. A fact she had no complaints about.

"Yay. You're still here," Fiona said, placing goodies on the counter.

It was funny how her friend was so in tune with Kaydee's stomach.

"Bless you." She grinned, snagging her iced coffee and chocolate chip muffin. "How'd you know I needed a pick-me-up?"

The much-needed fuel was perfect for tackling the

next chore on Kaydee's list of repairs. Between her side of the house and her grandfather's side, the list seemed never-ending. And this was *after* her grandfather had already tackled their first list. Granted, that list had been shorter and less labor-intensive. Now the second list needed attention. If she undertook one repair a day, she'd eventually cross them all off.

"What's on your agenda today?" Fiona asked, flipping her auburn mane over her shoulder before biting into her muffin.

"The rail that separates our steps out front," she replied, heading back to clean her station. "It's very shaky, and I'm worried someone might get hurt."

"Like your grandfather?"

"No. Me." She chuckled, setting her drink down, but not her muffin. She had plans for that delicious thing. "You know how sure-footed I am."

Fiona snickered. "Yes, 'graceful' is *so* not your middle name."

She laughed. "No, that would be 'klutz' or 'gimp,' depending on if it's before or after I trip over my own feet."

"Is there a reason you waited until today to tackle that particular repair?" Fiona asked, twisting around to lean her butt against Kaydee's counter. "A certain blue-eyed, long-haired, sexy former Army Ranger, perhaps?"

Fiona had met Leo on several occasions at Ava's house and was always quick to point out their crazy chemistry. Popping the rest of her muffin into her mouth, Kaydee gave Fiona her best innocent look.

Her friend's green gaze twinkled. "Leo *is* coming up to check on Ava today, right? So...repairing the porch should ensure you won't miss your hot-guy sighting."

Since that had been her plan all week, Kaydee didn't bother to deny it. Mostly because heat rushed into her face and gave her away. "Can't blame me."

"Hell no." Fiona chuckled, then pointed at her with her muffin. "But I *do* blame you for not making a move on that delicious man months ago."

She grabbed a broom and began to sweep the floor around her station. "Wrong timing."

Her life had been just this side of out-of-control when they first met. Between finding a place for her and her grandfather to live, giving up the lease on her condo, and moving her grandfather from his one-bedroom apartment, she was beyond taxed. And settling in those first few months was an adjustment, too. It was a miracle if she remembered to brush her teeth in the morning. So, yeah, dating had been out of the question.

But now... An image of Leo flashed through Kaydee's mind, with his startling blue eyes, amazing smile, and that mop of dark hair she longed to grip while kissing the breath from his gorgeous, mouthwatering body.

Yearning quivered through her.

Fiona chuckled. "Uh-huh. How's that timing now?"

A smile tugged her lips. "Better."

"So does that mean you're finally going to go after him?"

She finished cleaning up, then put the broom against the wall. "Maybe." She shrugged, her mind drifting back to her childhood. "You know I'm not all that good at making the first move."

Fiona snickered. "Honey, trust me, all you have to do is bat your eyelashes at that man and he's yours."

"Exaggerate much?" She laughed, grabbing her drink and purse from her station.

"Nope. True story."

If only. She shook her head. "Doesn't matter, since I'd have to get up the courage to do that, and I'd probably end up looking like I got something in my eye."

"Also a true story."

"Yep." She nodded toward the front of the shop, ready to change the subject. "Looks like your two o'clock is here, and I should get going. See you tomorrow."

For the better part of her half-hour commute home, Kaydee's thoughts remained on Leo, and her friend's words.

Honey, trust me, all you have to do is bat your eyelashes at that man and he's yours.

Leo *had* seemed a little friendlier last Friday. Could her friend be right?

Invisible butterflies swarmed her belly. Maybe. But she refused to stress over it. The afternoon's to-do list required her full attention, starting with making sure her grandfather ate something good. By the time she parked in her driveway, she had her head screwed back on straight, a meal planned for dinner, and a determination to fix the railing.

After checking on her grandfather, she changed into jeans and a T-shirt, pulled her hair into a ponytail, then threw a load of clothes in the wash. One of her least favorite chores, but like the others, it was a necessity.

On her way to the door, she grabbed her toolbox and pink tool belt from the closet, secured the tool belt around her hips, then headed outside.

Maybe this once, her chore would go off without a hitch.

Sending a fervent wish that the repair gods were in a good mood today, Kaydee set the toolbox on the porch and inhaled slowly. She had a better chance of hitting the lotto. Exhaling, she tugged the railing that extended from the half wall that separated the sides of the porch down to the bottom step. It wobbled back and forth while she examined it from top to bottom, and end to end. Not too bad. She needed to nail the top and bottom rails more securely to the end posts.

Easy peasy. She hoped.

Grabbing a long nail from one of the front pouches and

her hammer from a ring, Kaydee's mind drifted to Leo. Would he show up today? It was possible he got tied up at the ranch or stuck in traffic. Not that it mattered. It wasn't like she was going to take Fiona's advice and make a move or anything.

She lined up the nail, drew her hammer back, and swung.

"Hey, Kaydee."

Leo's low timbre hit her ears a second before her hammer missed the nail completely and struck her thumb.

Son of a BB gun.

Dropping the hammer, she shook her hand, hoping to alleviate the throbbing in her thumb. "Hey, Leo," she said, turning around.

"Sorry." Brow creased in concern, he took the steps two at a time and stopped at her side. "I thought you heard me coming."

Hell, she hadn't even heard his truck pull in across the street. Because her mind was too preoccupied...with thoughts of him.

Her thumb throbbed like nobody's business until Leo grasped her hand and kissed it.

And just like that the universe stopped, or maybe just the space around them, because the world faded away, leaving her in a warm bubble with her fantasy man. The feel of his lips brushing her skin was as unexpected as it was amazing. In the next instant, her thumping pain eased, and her heartbeats quickened. Kaydee lifted her gaze from Leo's mouth to stare into his fathomless blue eyes that darkened to a sexy cobalt hue. Unable to move, and barely able to breath, she watched his gaze drop to her lips.

Holy...

Anticipation rushed through her body, and her still-thudding heart rocked in her chest.

He was going to kiss her.

Chapter Three

"Hey, Leo." Her grandfather stepped out of his house and broke the spell. "How was your drive up?"

Leo blinked, and the heat immediately disappeared from his gaze. "Good," he replied, releasing her hand before turning his attention to her grandfather. "I must've just beat the rush."

Her grandfather chuckled. "That's like hitting the lotto."

"I know," Leo said with a grin.

Needing a moment to regain her composure, Kaydee bent down to retrieve her hammer. For her, hitting the lotto would've been that kiss she just missed out on.

"Would you like a beer?" her grandfather asked, settling into his favorite porch chair.

Leo nodded. "Sure."

She straightened and frowned at her grandfather. "You don't have any."

"I know. But you do." The conniver smirked. "So when you fetch Leo a beer, would you bring me one, too?"

She snickered. "You're incorrigible."

"But you love me anyway."

Smiling, she provided the long-standing response she'd given the wonderful man since her childhood. "Only times infinity. But just so you know, I'm only doing this because I need to go inside to flip my laundry."

With the smile still lingering, she headed to her door, and her joy increased as the wonderful sound of Leo's laughter followed her inside. He didn't laugh nearly enough. Oh, the guy chuckled and grinned for sure, but an honest-to-goodness laugh? That was rare. And a gift. Leo needed to loosen up more and laugh often.

Once she finished flipping the laundry, she opened her fridge and grabbed three beers.

She needed one, too. Big-time. For some reason, her mouth was dry.

After she opened the bottles, she stepped out onto her porch to find Leo fixing the railing. "You don't need to do that."

"I know." He glanced up at her from the bottom of the steps and smiled. "I want to. And it's no big deal. It's what I do."

"Yeah, at your day job," she said. "You shouldn't have to do it during your downtime."

His smile widened. "I don't mind. I enjoy it." He lifted his hand, and that's when she noticed he held a drill, and a large toolbox sat near his feet.

He must've fetched them from his truck when she was inside.

"Thanks for the beer. Can you put it on the porch? I'll have it in a few minutes."

"Of course." She handed her grandfather his beer, then pointed at his drill. "So...nails weren't the best choice to fix the rail?"

He shook his head. "No. Too much give. Screws are more

secure and provide a better anchor."

Kaydee made a mental note of it...and of the way his T-shirt stretched across broad shoulders and muscles rippled across his back. Maybe she'd hit the lottery, after all. Someone was fixing the rail for her and looked great doing it. Settling down on the top step, she sipped her beer and enjoyed the view for several glorious minutes.

But all too soon, he was straightening up and putting away his tools.

"Thanks, Leo," her grandfather said. "You coming back this weekend?"

Kaydee found herself holding her breath, although she was pretty certain he was driving up.

"Yeah. Why?"

"Toolbox coming with you?"

Leo chuckled. "Yes, sir. Is there something else you need me to work on?"

"A few things could use fixing," her grandfather replied. "Kaydee's done a fine job, but the stuff that's left requires someone with more expertise."

"Make a list, and I'd be happy to help."

Kaydee's heart cracked open, and a wave of warmth flooded her chest. She was touched by his eagerness to help, but she didn't want him to work on his time off. "Thanks, Leo," she said, placing her beer down before rising to her feet. "But we can't monopolize your free time or take you away from visiting your grandmother."

"It's fine," he said. "I'm still keeping my promise to my mom, but you know my grandmother. Do you think she wants me hovering over her every minute?"

A smile tugged her lips. "No." Ava was too independent for that.

Her grandfather chuckled. "More like a capital *Hell No*."

"Exactly." Leo laughed as his gaze met hers. "So you see?

Helping you with repairs will give me something to do while I'm still close enough to keep my word to my mom."

He's also going to be close by me, her mind noted. A thrill shot down her spine.

"It's settled, then." Her grandfather grinned. "Thanks, Leo. I'll have my list ready by the weekend."

Nodding, Leo shifted his attention to her. "What about you? Is there anything I can help you with?"

Kaydee blinked and tried her hardest to keep from saying *me*. Not only was it inappropriate, it was improbable. And as much as she'd love to let him take over her to-do list, she still didn't feel right about making him work on his time off. "Thanks, but I'll manage."

"Nonsense," her grandfather muttered. "Let Leo fix the place. I'll spring for the material, and you can make him dinner or give him a years' worth of free haircuts or something. How's that sound to you, Leo?"

He smiled. "Great."

Her grandfather smiled. "Excellent. Now, if you'll excuse me, I need to wash up before we head over to Ava's. I hope you don't mind, but she's invited us over for dinner, too."

Leo's grin widened. "Nope. That's fine."

She bit her lip to keep from smirking. It was so cute how eager her grandfather was to spend time with their neighbor.

After the smitten senior disappeared into his house, Leo turned to her. "You don't need to cook for me or cut my hair, Kaydee. I'm happy to help out."

More of that warmth funneled through her chest. "Thanks. That's sweet, but I can't let you work without getting paid. So, this railing." She grasped it and tugged. No wobbling. It didn't budge. "Just tell me what you want for fixing it."

A brow quirked above his devilish gaze.

"I-I didn't mean that like it sounded." Heat rushed into

her cheeks. And damn, she couldn't stop a brief vision of them naked and rolling in her sheets from flashing through her mind.

A sexy grin tugged his lips. He knew.

Dammit.

"Tell you what." He picked up their drinks and handed hers to her. "How about we enjoy our beers and call it good?"

"Okay. This time." She returned his smile, but when she reached for her beer, her fingers brushed his palm. Their gazes meet, and the universe disappeared again.

What was with that? Unsure what to do, especially since he didn't act on the heat flaring in his eyes, she broke contact and sipped her beer.

Getting involved with him was playing with fire.

Trouble was, her life lacked fire.

• • •

Later that night, Leo returned to the ranch with several things on his mind. First and foremost was Kaydee. No matter how hard he tried, he couldn't get the damn woman out of his mind. And the more time he spent with her the more she lingered in his head. Good or bad? The jury was still out on that one. But he did know he liked touching her. A lot. Too much. He found that out when he screwed up that afternoon and caused her to hurt herself.

Getting out of his truck, he muttered a curse and slammed the door. He hadn't meant to startle her today. Hell, he hadn't exactly been quiet, and yet when he'd spoken, the poor woman jumped and whacked her thumb with a hammer. Leo knew firsthand that hurt like a son of a bitch. He hated that he caused her so much pain.

She insisted she was fine, but he could tell by her dilated eyes and tight lips that she was hurting. Overcome with the urge to erase that look from her face, he'd unthinkingly grasped her hand and kissed her thumb. The act—which felt as natural as breathing—was so out of character for him. He didn't recognize himself, but he *did* recognize how his body reacted to the feel of her skin. She was soft and warm and smelled like raspberries. His whole body immediately sprang to life. It was an awakening of sorts, and again, he wasn't sure if it was good or bad.

The image of her gorgeous brown eyes and how they widened with the same damn awareness rushing through him flashed through his head. He always knew Kaydee was special, so of course touching her would be, too. If Nate hadn't come out of the house when he had, Leo would've discovered how she tasted as well. He'd wondered about it for several damn months now. The interruption was probably for the best, though.

"Are you going to stand in the driveway all night?" Stone asked from his perch on one of the porch chairs.

Leo hadn't even seen him sitting there, or Vince. Hell, either the porch light was too dim…or he was.

Probably the latter.

"My guess is the answer's yes," Vince said, lopsided grin on his face. "He's too busy smiling to move."

He was smiling? With a shake of his head, he stepped onto the porch, leaned against a post, and folded his arms. "You two done yet?"

"Hmm." Stone rubbed his jaw. "Wonder who put that smile there?" he asked as if Leo hadn't spoken.

He cocked his chin. "Hey, I smile."

Stone snorted. "Yeah, if you have gas."

"Or ate one of Emma's pies." Vince grinned.

"Still smiles, so they count."

Vince tipped his head and narrowed his gaze. "Well, you weren't here for Emma's pie tonight, and we don't need to fumigate the place, so…?"

He shrugged. "So, what?"

"So, you're saying your visits to Dallas are just to see your grandmother?" Stone asked.

Leo unfolded his arms and held the man's stare. "Yes. I told you I wanted keep an eye on her while my mom's away, remember?"

Vince's brow rose over an amused gaze. "You're busted, pal. We've been in your shoes. We know the signs. Don't even try to tell us a girl isn't the reason for the visits."

"No." His lips twitched. "But she is an added bonus."

"Added bonuses are good," Stone said.

"No, they're great," Vince said. "I should know. I discovered that firsthand with Emma."

His buddy was right. Vince's stint as Emma's pretend boyfriend had turned into the real deal, and he attributed that to their killer chemistry. Kind of like what Leo had with Kaydee. Not that he was about to admit that to the two smiling idiots.

Time to change the subject to the other thought on his mind. "So, Stone, I've been thinking."

"That's dangerous," Vince muttered good-naturedly.

Leo *good-naturedly* flipped him off.

"About what?" Stone asked.

"About your offer to build me a house on this ranch." The more he thought about it, the more he knew what he wanted to do. He loved the ranch and helping men and women who had a tough time fitting back into society. Like he did. But he'd changed. It was time to show it. "I'm interested, but only on one condition."

"What's that?"

"That you let me buy into the ranch and business like the others." He held his friend's gaze. If he saw any sign of pity, or anything similar, he was gone. He wasn't looking for a handout.

"Done."

Leo blinked. "Done?"

"Yeah, done," Vince echoed.

He frowned, bouncing his gaze between the two men. "But don't you have to talk it out with Brick and Cord? I should've called a meeting."

"No need," Stone said. "We've already had this discussion."

Vince grinned. "Yeah, we were just waiting for you to bring it up."

"No shit?"

Stone grinned, too. "No shit." He rose to his feet and held out his hand. "Welcome aboard."

Leo hesitated. "Wait. I need to know how much everyone contributed."

"Not everyone put in the same amount," Stone said.

"Yeah," Vince said. "Cord and I had family obligations that ate into our savings, but we put in what we could."

A ripple of relief washed over Leo. "I have a good chunk now. A few more months and I'll have more saved up. But until then, I don't feel comfortable doing anything."

Stone nodded, his hand still stretched out. "Deal."

"Deal." A smile tugged at Leo's lips, and as he shook Stone's hand, an emotion he hadn't felt in a long time rippled through him.

Pride.

Years of self-doubt and loathing had blocked any appearance of positive emotions. It felt good, *damn* good, to have his body riddled with them for a change.

"Yeah, welcome aboard, Leo." Vince stepped close to shake hands.

"Thanks, but I'm not aboard until I get all the money together." He released Vince's hand and stared at Stone.

"And hold my own like Vince and the others." He needed to prove to everyone that he was back on his feet and reliable again.

"Then I think it's time you had your own crew," Stone said. "You already proved you can handle the position when you covered for Vince last summer. I've just been waiting for you to ask." The smile on Stone's face was brighter than the dim porch light. "I have a kitchen remodel lined up to start on Monday. You want it?"

Hell yeah. "Thanks. I don't know what to say." The fact that his buddy thought so highly of him, after all his poor choices, was damn humbling.

"Say yes."

"Yes."

God, he hadn't realized how much he'd missed being regarded as a valued member of the team. But even through all his trials and tribulations since leaving active duty, none of them ever turned their backs on him. He owed his friends everything. Especially Stone.

Leo just hoped he didn't let his buddy down.

Chapter Four

On Friday, Kaydee put in an extra shift at work to cover for Rose when her boss called to tell them she wasn't coming in. Thankfully, she'd had just enough time to make it home to pick up her grandfather and Ava and drop them off at the rec center for bingo night.

"Thank you, dear," her neighbor said. "Leo's on his way but stuck in that dang traffic. I told him not to worry, you had us covered."

"Anytime." She smiled, not because she just found out Leo was on his way. Nope. The smile was nothing more than a polite gesture to her friend.

That was her story and she was sticking to it.

"You wouldn't have to take us if you'd let me drive, Kaydee."

She met her grandfather's gaze in the rearview mirror. "If it wasn't going to be dark when bingo was over, then you know I would've let you."

They had this same argument every week.

He rolled his eyes. "I had one scrape."

Kaydee sighed. "Three, Grandpa. You had three." And she was damn glad he'd been able to walk away from the last accident with just a broken wrist.

"If it weren't for that damn dog running out in front of me, I wouldn't have swerved and hit the stupid tree." He folded his arms across his chest and grumbled.

"I hate when that happens," Ava said. "Ever play chicken with a goat? I did. Damn thing charged right down the middle of Pickler Road straight at me."

Kaydee glanced sideways at the woman, unsure if she was pulling their legs. But her gaze was serious. "What'd you do?"

"Swerved, like Nate," Ava said. "Only, I didn't hit a tree. I took out a section of Old Man Turner's fence. He was right pissed about it, too." The woman chuckled. "But seeing as it was his goat that was loose, he didn't have a leg to stand on."

"Or four," her grandfather added from the back seat.

The three of them were still laughing when Kaydee pulled into the rec center parking lot.

"We'll see you in two hours," Ava said, opening the door. "Oh, and I left chicken for you and Leo in the Crock-Pot. Enjoy."

Apparently, she was having dinner with Leo at his grandmother's house. Alone. Her heart skipped a beat as she drove home. Would he think she engineered it? She hoped not. Not that she didn't want to have dinner with him. She did. Very much. But she'd never orchestrate it so deviously.

Anxiety choked the life out of her glee.

What if he didn't want company? Poor guy probably had another physical day at work and was no doubt exhausted. Last thing he needed was his grandmother's neighbor pushing herself on him.

Maybe she'd get home before he arrived and could just slip into her house unnoticed. Leo was more than capable of feeding himself. Yeah. That was what she'd do.

Relief and disappointment mixed when Kaydee parked at her house and noted no truck in Ava's driveway. She had gotten home before Leo arrived. Getting out of her car, she clung to the relief and used it as a shield to ward off disappointment. She didn't need any more complications in her life. Work was complex enough.

With that thought in mind, she'd just reached her sidewalk when Leo honked his horn and pulled into Ava's driveway. Her pulse hiccuped. He got out and headed her way.

So much for getting inside before he arrived.

"Hey, Kaydee," he said as he crossed the street. Something was up. Something was different. In a good way. His stride was a little more confident than normal. He appeared taller. "Thanks for taking my grandmother."

"Of course." She smiled and pretended the heat flooding her cheeks was caused by the evening sun. "I usually take the two of them anyway. You really don't need to rush up here on Fridays for that."

Traffic was horrible. She didn't wish it on anyone.

"Thanks. I appreciate it, but I don't mind." He stopped in front of her and his smile and gaze were...well, brighter. Stronger.

She blinked, trying to figure out what was different.

"And forget about going home," he said. "My grandmother already instructed me to feed you. She apparently has dinner in the Crock-Pot for the both of us."

Kaydee snickered. Leave it to Ava. "So I've been told."

"Then come on, let's eat." He motioned toward his grandmother's house, that sexy smile still lingering on his lips.

Was she staring? She couldn't help it. He had great lips. They were full and talented...at least they were talented in her many fantasies.

Realizing he was waiting for her reply, she regained

control of her wits and returned his grin. "Yes, sir." She saluted before crossing the quiet street.

Yeah, something was definitely different. When they reached his grandmother's sidewalk, he fell into step alongside her. She glanced sideways at him from under her lashes. He was still smiling. It was a record. Leo never held a smile for longer than a few seconds. This was going on two minutes.

Once inside the house, she continued into the kitchen, trying to come up with something to say. "This is your grandmother's place. Not mine. I should be following you."

He snickered from behind. "As if she'd mind."

"True." She chuckled.

Ava was a firm believer in get-it-yourself-you-know-where-it-is.

Leo grabbed dishes for them from the cupboard and placed them next to the Crock-Pot, while she fetched the silverware and set it on the table.

"What would you like to drink?"

Drinks? He was getting them drinks?

She turned to face him. "All right. What gives? I'm dying of curiosity, Leo. Why are you so happy?"

"Water it is." He swiped two bottles from the fridge and deposited them on the table next to their silverware. "Are you saying I'm never happy?"

"No." She eyed him carefully, trying to assess what was going on behind his mischievous gaze. "But something has definitely happened since I saw you on Wednesday."

He straightened up and smiled even wider. "I've been given my own crew. Start our first job on Monday."

"That's wonderful, Leo!" Without thinking, she launched herself at him. His grandmother had confided in her how hard he'd been working the past year, and how important it was to him to pull his own weight both at the ranch and at work. "Congratulations." She wrapped her arms around him and squeezed tight. He deserved something good to happen to him.

"Thanks," he rumbled, banding his arms around her tight.

The feel of all that lean, hard muscle stole her breath. All of a sudden, her joy for him turned to something a lot hotter as awareness surged through her body in wave after wave of heat.

That was new.

He must've felt it, too, because he stilled and drew back just enough to hold her gaze. "You're not making this easy."

"M-making what easy?"

"Resisting you."

Well hell, he wasn't making things easy, either. She already liked him. A lot. That could prove problematic when she was free to leave.

But that was two years from now. A lot could happen in two years.

With her heart pounding a crazy beat in her chest, she tipped her head and decided to take a chance. "What if I don't want you to?"

Something flashed through his eyes, an aching hunger that matched her own. Muttering an oath, he stepped back into her personal space.

The butterflies in her stomach fluttered to life, then swarmed up a storm as she watched his mouth slowly lower to hers. For a split second they shared a breath before he covered her lips with his in a knee-weakening kiss she felt to the tips of her hair.

As if wanting to savor her, he inched his hands up her arms, over her throat, to caress her jaw with his thumbs. Unexpected and amazing, a current surged through her, tingling her body to life. She had the goose bumps to prove it. He tipped her face and deepened the kiss.

Damn, he was a good kisser. The best. She ran her hands up his chest, over his shoulders to hold tight, enjoying the feel of his solid strength against her curves. He was hot and hard, and it was weird how her whole body softened because of it. Taking his time, he sampled and tasted, teasing her lips with his tongue until she almost whimpered. But she wasn't a whimperer.

She wasn't much of anything when it came to sex. Oh, she enjoyed it, but it usually took her a while to get there.

It wouldn't with Leo, if his kiss was anything to go by. Need vibrated through her, and she was mere seconds away from melting into him. If it weren't for needing oxygen, she never wanted it to end.

Just when she was about to pass out, Leo broke the kiss, setting his forehead against hers while he sucked in air. Doing the same, she tried to make sense of what just happened.

It wasn't as if she'd never been kissed. Goodness, she'd had her fair share, but this one was exceptional. More than her mouth was engaged. It was as if her whole body jolted to life.

"Damn, Kaydee." Still breathing heavy, he drew back enough for her to note that his blue gaze was dark and hungry. "I've wanted to do that for a long time now."

"Me, too." She slid her hands from his shoulders up into his gorgeous hair, loving the feel of the soft strands on her fingers. Such a contradiction to his hard body. "I've also wanted to do this," she said, tugging his head down until their lips met again.

Back and forth, she teased and drank, giving his mouth the same treatment he gave hers a minute ago. Kaydee didn't know what prompted Leo to finally make a move, but damn, she was glad he had.

So damn glad.

Apparently, he was, too, because he slid one hand up her

back and used the other to hold her head at an angle while he swept his tongue inside her mouth, and proceeded to drive her wild.

Over and over he explored, and she explored, too, brushing his tongue with hers, eager to learn his taste, his likes, and his loves. She simultaneously touched his tongue and the roof of his mouth. He let out a groan and crushed her closer.

A *love*. Definitely a love.

Empowered by that knowledge, she gladly met him stroke for stroke. He was a master, and she desperately wanted to climb up his body to feel more of him. She needed more.

But once again, lack of air had them drawing back and inhaling while their foreheads met. Spurts of hot air hit her face as she worked to regain control and she tried to remove the fog from her brain.

If someone told her that morning that she'd make out with Leo in his grandmother's kitchen that evening she would've called them crazy. And yet she had just kissed Leo. Twice. In his grandmother's kitchen.

Who was the crazy one now?

Reeling from the intensity of what just happened, Kaydee blinked. "That was even better than the first one."

"Makes me wonder if they'll keep getting better and better." A slow, sexy grin curved his lips. "Care to test that theory?"

With her heart skipping another beat, she sent him an answering smile. "Perhaps we should."

Leo slowly pulled her to him and took her lips in another brain cell–zapping kiss that had her fisting his shirt to keep from falling. This was crazy, and amazing, and she was happy to go insane with him. Pressing closer, she opened her mouth under his, loving the way he immediately dipped his tongue inside. With another low, sexy sound emanating from his throat, he kissed her slow and deliciously deep.

It was official. Kaydee couldn't feel her legs. They turned to goo. This was her first time experiencing kiss-induced goo-for-legs.

She liked it. A lot.

Perhaps too much. Because there was no way she could go back to being just an acquaintance or friend to Leo.

Not after experiencing his mind-blowing kisses.

But what if he didn't want to be more than friends?

His body stiffened up a second before he broke the kiss.

Maybe he regretted everything. Maybe he wasn't ready to let go like he had. Or maybe he wasn't stiffening up. Maybe he was just hard all over, because he was…hard…all over. Heat pooled low in her belly and did nothing to alleviate her need for more of him.

But did he need more of her? Or more important, did he *want* more of her? Kaydee wasn't sure, and his neutral expression gave nothing away.

• • •

This wasn't the first time in Leo's life that he'd lost his senses, but it was the first time he'd lost them while sober. Intoxication was definitely involved, though. And her name was Kaydee. Damn. She tasted even better than he'd imagined. Sweet and lush like a ripe strawberry, and hot as hell.

She rocked his world.

All through a kiss. Several kisses, because he couldn't seem to help himself. The delicious woman was dangerous to his self-control. Still, what was the harm? She appeared to enjoy it as much as he had.

Her face was flushed, her lips were swollen and wet, and her ample chest rose and fell rapidly with her ragged breaths. As he stared into her gorgeous eyes, dark with the same desire still flowing through his veins, an unexpected thrill flooded his chest.

He put that sexy look on her face.

"So…that just happened," she uttered between breaths, sending a piece of hair across her cheek.

He nodded. "Yes."

"Can you explain to me what that was?"

"No." His lips twitched as he pushed the strand off her face with his finger and hooked it behind her ear. "I was hoping you could tell me."

It felt as if he'd gotten knocked on his ass.

She released her death grip on his shirt and smoothed the material with her palms. "I would if I could, but I can't, so I won't."

Leo laughed. Kaydee had such an honest, spontaneous, lighthearted way that always put him at ease. It was her superpower. The amazing woman had pulled more laughs from him in the past few months than he'd had in the last two years. She was magical. Addicting.

Trouble.

Her gaze dropped to his mouth, and he watched her pull her plump lower lip between her teeth. His damn dick twitched in response.

He was so fucking screwed.

Releasing her, he cleared his dry-as-hell throat and stepped back. "We should probably eat."

Especially since supper wasn't the root of his hunger.

She blinked and gave her head a slight shake. "You're right." As her gaze cleared, a grin curved her lips. "If we don't put a dent in that Crock-Pot meal we'll suffer the wrath of Ava."

"True." He laughed again. "We don't want that."

But he *did* want Kaydee. Hell, he wanted her before they'd kissed. But now that he tasted her, Leo knew it was only a matter of time before they ended up in bed. Kaydee's hunger was intense and matched his own. It was inevitable.

A fact that both thrilled and scared the hell out of him.

And if he didn't focus on something else, he was going to burst and make a fool out of himself in the middle of his grandmother's kitchen. So when they sat down to eat and she asked what his new position entailed, he gladly answered. Before long, he was asking questions, too. Personal ones. Something he'd never done with a woman before.

Kaydee was full of firsts for him.

"Where did you live before moving here?"

"In a condo near Fort Worth," she replied, a wistful smile curving her lips. "It had two bedrooms and one and a half baths. I tried to convince my grandfather to move in with me, but he's too independent. He didn't want a roommate. And even if he did, and wanted to keep his apartment, I couldn't stay with him because he only had one bedroom. So he purchased the duplex in his neighborhood and asked me to move in to the other side. Of course I broke my lease and moved in. It's actually a good setup. He has his privacy, but I can still keep an eye on him."

Leo frowned. Nate seemed fine to him. "Why do you need to keep an eye on him?"

"He can't drive at night, but he won't admit it, and he's gotten in a few fender benders because of it," she replied. "Plus, he has blood sugar issues. My parents are worried about him being on his own. Especially when he was living here in Dallas. It was too far from me during rush hours and stuff if there was an emergency. And he refused to move to California where my dad's stationed until he retires in two years."

Leo started to get the whole picture. "So you offered to look after him until they move back to Texas."

"Yes." She smiled, and it did funny things to his chest.

"It's only two years. And I like this area. It has some really great perks."

Her gaze was warm and open, and a pretty blush filled her cheeks. She meant him, and surprisingly, he was all right with that. The urge to flee never materialized.

"I'm glad you moved here. I think you're amazing," he said. "You gave up your place and your privacy to help your grandfather out."

Her selflessness was refreshing.

She shrugged and dropped her gaze to her empty plate. "If I was so amazing, I would've found a place to rent close to his apartment instead of making him move. But it was his idea. In fact, he was the one who insisted on buying the duplex and moving here." Her gaze rounded. "I'm sorry. I can't believe I just told you all of that."

He smiled. "It's okay. I'm glad you did."

He was also glad she moved into his grandmother's neighborhood. Kaydee clearly thought she was being selfish, but what he saw was a woman trying to please everyone. She was caring and strong, and it added to her appeal.

A hell of a lot.

The brick wall shielding his heart cracked open enough for her to reach him. Any chance he might've had of fighting his attraction to her just bit the dust. But it was okay. He just needed to keep things light and fun so he didn't hurt her.

Or himself.

Because once she found out about his past, this thing between them—whatever it was—would be over. And she would find out. It was only a matter of time.

Chapter Five

Midmorning on Monday, Kaydee sat in the coffee shop next to the salon enjoying a cup with Fiona. Her friend had to work that morning, but Kaydee didn't go in until later that afternoon, which meant she got to check out the next prospective property alone.

"You know what? I just had a great idea," Fiona said, devious grin spreading across her face.

Kaydee's insides cringed. "Uh-oh. Whatever it is, my answer is no."

"But you don't even know what it is yet."

"Don't need to." She shook her head. Hard. "I've seen that look too many times before, and always paid the price."

Fiona cocked her head. "Are you still sore about that surprise party?"

She frowned. "Surprise party? You told me it was a costume party." She swiped her phone off the table, thumbed through her photos until she found the one she wanted, then shoved it front of her friend's nose. "I showed up dressed like Wonder Woman, remember?"

"That *was* the surprise." Fiona laughed. "But you looked amazing, and it got you two dates, didn't it?"

A smile tugged Kaydee's lips. "True." She put her phone down. "Although I could've done without Mr. *Groper*. He had more hands than an octopus."

"An octopus doesn't have hands."

She groaned. "You know what I mean."

Fiona laughed. "I also know that none of those dates matter now that you have Leo."

Kaydee's heart fluttered in her chest. "I don't *have* Leo. We're just friends." She almost got away with that statement, but heat rushed into her cheeks.

"Friends my ass." Fiona's gaze narrowed. "Just what did he work on this weekend? You or your house?"

Both. "The house, of course."

"Are you trying to tell me you two didn't kiss?"

She lifted her chin. "I didn't say that." Her blush took away any chance she had of keeping that secret from her friend. Good thing she didn't want to keep it a secret.

"Yeah?" Fiona leaned closer. "How was it?"

"Wonderful." She sighed as the memory of his mind-boggling kisses warmed her from head to toe. "It was as if the world just faded away. I didn't think brain fog was real until he kissed me."

"So…he kissed you more than once?"

She nodded.

"How many times?"

Not nearly enough. She lifted a shoulder. "I don't know. A couple on Friday. A few more on Saturday, and once yesterday, before he left."

Each time, they were more and more amazing. If his grandmother hadn't been on the porch with her grandfather, she would've invited him to her place last night. Hell, she would've grabbed his hand and tugged him across the street straight into her house so she could give in to the urge to climb his body. Naked.

"Then my idea is spot-on," Fiona said, bringing Kaydee's mind back to the present.

She bit her tongue for a full thirty seconds before giving in. "Okay, what idea?"

"Since the building you're checking out for me today is halfway between here and Joyful, why don't you invite Leo to lunch?"

She widened her eyes. "I couldn't do that."

"Why not?"

"Because…it's…I… What if he doesn't want to?" she finally said. "He started his new job today. I think they're ripping things out or something. I don't want to seem like a pest."

Or pushy. Kaydee really liked Leo and was warming up to the idea of having some fun with him. Two years in Dallas could be a lot more fun with him in it. Last thing she wanted was to ruin that prospect.

"Honey, the man kissed you every day for the past three days. You are not a pest. You're an obsession. Trust me. New job or not, he'll want to see you."

The property she was viewing for Fiona was about thirty-five miles south of town, which made it thirty minutes north of Joyful. "I don't know, Fi. I'm not the type to put myself out there."

"Isn't Leo different? Isn't he worth taking that chance?" her friend asked, pushing Kaydee's phone closer. "Go on. Call him."

Could it be that simple? Was her friend right? Would Leo actually agree?

Even though the possibility was slight, Kaydee decided she couldn't pass it up. "Okay. I'll do it. But I'm going to text him instead." She couldn't bear to hear him reject her. It'd be easier to read. Right? Gathering courage, she scrolled through her contacts until his number appeared. They'd exchanged them months ago, in case she needed to contact him about his grandmother.

Only, this had nothing to do with Ava.

Before she lost her nerve, Kaydee typed out a quick explanation about her visit to Lansbury, asked him to lunch, then hit send. "Oh my God. I can't believe I just did that! Is there a way I could stop it?"

"No." Fiona chuckled, wiggling the phone from Kaydee's grasp before putting it on the table. "It'll be okay. He's going to accept. Trust me."

When a whole minute went by without a response, the nervousness fluttering through her stomach turned into a tight knot. "Dammit. I shouldn't have done that. Now he's trying to come up with a way to turn me down."

"You don't know that," Fiona insisted. "Give him a few minutes. He's at work, remember? It's not like he can just stop in the middle of busting things out."

She sighed. "True."

But the bravado rushing through her a few minutes ago was gone, leaving her full of uncertainty. What in the world had she been thinking?

Before she could form an answer, her phone dinged with a text.

Her pulse hiccuped. Leo actually responded. She met her friend's gaze for a second, then picked up her phone and read the text.

Do you know where the Lansbury Diner is? I can meet you at noon.

Her stomach fluttered as if she'd suddenly swallowed a whole swarm of butterflies.

Yes. I'll see you there, she responded.

"Well?" Anticipation vibrated through her friend's tone.

"What did he say?"

Kaydee couldn't stop the smile from tugging her lips. "We're meeting in two hours." Which was perfect, since her appointment with the Realtor wasn't until one thirty.

Fiona patted her hand. "See? Aren't you glad you took the chance?"

She blew out a breath and nodded but wasn't sure she'd have the guts do it again.

Unless, of course, lunch went well.

• • •

To say Leo was surprised was the understatement of the year. He'd never expected Kaydee to text him, let alone invite him to lunch. But more surprising than that had been his acceptance. He never even thought to decline.

And considering how much he had enjoyed the past forty minutes of her company that afternoon, he was glad he had accepted. A thought that reverberated through his mind as they left the diner and he walked her to her vehicle.

"So, where are you off to now?" he asked, stalling by her car, reluctant to go, even though he needed to get back to work. His first day as a supervisor was probably best spent supervising.

"I'm supposed to meet the realtor a few streets from here," she said, stopping at her door before turning to face him. "Thank you for taking time out of your first day to meet me."

He smiled. He couldn't help it. "Thanks for the invite."

She stepped toward him, and he stood transfixed as he watched the color rise into her pretty face, deepening the brown of her mesmerizing eyes. The woman was adorable, and her open, hopeful gaze warmed his heart. A foreign feeling he was willing to experience again. And again. But only with Kaydee. It was as if his heart were slowly thawing, coming back to life.

And when she placed her hands on his shoulders and lifted on tiptoe to brush her lips to his, a different organ woke up. One farther south. His favorite one.

The warmth she brought to his body instantly increased. He slid his hands around her back, but he let her control the kiss. Like the woman, it was tentative and sweet, and a turn-on unlike anything he'd ever experienced. But all too soon it ended, and she released him.

"So..." She cleared her throat and stepped back. "I guess I'll see you Wednesday...when you come up to visit your grandmother. You are coming up to visit her then, right?"

God, she really was adorable.

"Yes." He smiled and moved closer. He liked being close to her. Way too much. "What would you like me to work on?"

A flash of heat flickered through her gaze. "M-me...I mean...my side."

Holy shit. Leo's heart kicked the hell out of his ribs. He knew she was talking about her house and not offering herself, but damn. For a split second, he couldn't deny the rush of pure pleasure that washed through him.

This time, *he* cleared his throat. "Yeah, you," he said, brushing her soft cheek with his thumb. "I've been fixing things on your grandfather's side of the house. It's time I tackled something on your side."

Ever since he'd known her, Kaydee always put her grandfather's needs first. He admired the hell out of her for it. But now he wanted to do something for her. To scratch something off her to-do list.

She gave her head a little shake as if to clear it, something she seemed to do a lot around him. "M-my upstairs shower needs tiling."

He smiled. "I'll start working on that Wednesday evening."

"I...uh...can pitch in." She drew in a deep breath as if

oxygen-starved. "I'm off this Wednesday."

"Perfect. I'll see you then." And because he couldn't help himself, he leaned in and kissed her.

What was supposed to be a quick brush of lips swiftly morphed into a hot-as-hell embrace that had need canceling out all reason. Leo crushed Kaydee close, loving how she gripped his shoulders, as if he stole the strength from her legs.

Yeah, he liked that. A lot.

She tasted of tea and lemon, and if some asshole hadn't driven by blowing his horn and whistling out his window, Leo would've deepened the kiss. But she deserved better than him ravishing her in the middle of a damn parking lot.

With a reluctance he felt down to his steel-toed boots, he broke the kiss. "Sorry," he rumbled. "I can't seem to think straight with you in my arms."

"Ditto." Her warm, ragged breath washed over his neck. "You fog my brain."

Good.

His chest swelled. It'd been so long since any modicum of satisfaction paid him a visit.

"I should go." Kaydee pushed out of his arms and fumbled behind her for her door handle. "You need to get back to your crew, and I've…uh…got to see a guy…about a thing." She yanked her door open and dropped into the seat, as if maybe he really had stolen the strength from her legs. "Good luck with the rest of your first day."

"Thanks." He smiled. "I'll see you Wednesday."

And he was still smiling, twenty minutes later, when he parked at the job site. The woman was sweet and sexy at the same time, and the fact that she had no clue fueled the flame she ignited deep inside him.

But when he walked into the house, all thoughts of Kaydee disappeared, along with his smile.

What the hell?

Chapter Six

"Stop what you're doing!" Leo clenched his fists as he marched toward his crew. "You're busting out the wrong damn wall."

Dirk frowned, while two other crew members stiffened before turning to face him.

"What?" Tucker, the fourth crew member, scratched his temple. "We're removing the one you told us to take down."

"No." Leo shook his head, trying really hard not to lose his shit. "I told you to take *that* one down." He jabbed a finger toward the wall still intact. "Not this one. It's load bearing."

Thank God some of it was still there. Jesus, if he hadn't walked in when he had, they would've compromised the integrity of the whole damn second floor.

"But this is the one you told us to take down before you left," Dirk insisted.

Fuck.

Leo shoved a hand through his hair and gripped the back of his neck. Had he been unclear in his instructions? He ran the scene through his mind. Perhaps. That'd been right after Kaydee's lunch invitation.

Dammit. He should never have left.

"What do you want us to do?" Tucker asked as the others stared at him, waiting for orders.

Dirk blew out a breath. "Should we rebuild it?"

Leo glanced at the clock on the dining room wall and shook his head. "No. The Burmans will be here soon." It wasn't as if they could frame, drywall, spackle, and paint the damn thing in ten minutes. "Go to lunch. Take an hour."

Tucker stepped forward. "But we're the ones who screwed up. Not you. It's not fair that you should take the rap."

"It's okay, Tucker, and yes. I *am* to blame. I'm the supervisor, so I'm the one responsible. Go on and enjoy a good lunch. I'll take care of things here."

The kid hesitated a second before he left with the rest of the crew, who apologized to Leo as they walked by. He meant what he said to Tucker. It wasn't their fault.

It was his.

But it was time for solutions, not blame. Inhaling slowly, he glanced over the busted two-by-fours and Sheetrock in front of him and stared into the kitchen.

How could he fix this?

One of the requirements of being a Ranger was the ability to think on your feet. Something still ingrained in him. So within seconds, he formed an idea. With no time to waste, he pulled out the plans—the ones he should've shown his men before starting demolition—and sketched his idea, finishing just before the homeowners arrived.

After explaining the mix-up and shouldering the blame, Leo showed the clients his suggestion and quoted a new price. It was lower than it should be, but he'd cover the difference. He also gave the homeowners the option to stick with the original plan. He'd make sure their wall returned at no cost to them.

But in the end, the Burmans decided to go with the new

plan. They even thanked him and shook his hand. Leo knew he was a lucky son of a bitch. It could've gone so much worse and tarnished Foxtrot's name.

He hated that he'd put the company's reputation at risk. But what bothered him even more was almost letting Stone down.

The guy always had Leo's back, even when he didn't deserve it. And how did he repay him? By nearly blemishing what Stone and his buddies busted their asses to create for almost the past two years...on his first day as supervisor.

His first fucking day.

All because he'd let himself get distracted.

Stupid.

He never should've left the job site. Maybe he wasn't cut out to be a supervisor.

His chest tightened as his old friends—remorse and self-disgust—returned full force. He walked out to his truck, pulled the phone from his pocket, and stared at the screen.

It was time to do something even harder than facing the clients. It was time to tell Stone—a guy who believed in him, trusted him, always gave him the benefit of the doubt—that he'd screwed up. Again.

• • •

Wednesday afternoon couldn't come fast enough for Kaydee. Ever since her lunch with Leo on Monday, and those delicious kisses they'd shared in the parking lot, she'd thought of little else. Which was foolish. They weren't an item. Or even dating. So it was dumb to keep replaying the memories of them kissing through her mind.

And yet here she was, two days later, still thinking about them. She couldn't help herself. No one ever made her feel the way Leo did. With luck, maybe she had the same effect on him.

But when evening rolled around and there was still no sign of the guy, she decided to pull her hair back in a ponytail and start working on her upstairs bathroom.

Maybe he was stuck in traffic.

With her safety glasses in place, she stood in the middle of the tub and swung her hammer. Pieces of the hideous pink tile fell with a *clunk* into the tub, while a few smaller ones flew past her face. Good call not changing into shorts, but the tank top probably wasn't wise.

Maybe Leo got hung up at work.

She slammed the wall with her hammer again, and more tile fell into the tub. By the fourth swing, she realized the pieces didn't scatter if she held the neck of the hammer and didn't swing back as far.

Maybe she scared Leo off.

Her heart flopped in her chest, and she stilled the hammer in midair. What if he changed his mind? Decided they were better off keeping their friendship platonic?

Shoot. She exhaled and stared at the chipped wall in front of her. Kind of how she felt. Exposed. Layers removed. For the first time since her early childhood, she decided to take a chance, let her guard down...allow someone in. She was giving Leo the opportunity to get close and see the real her.

And he probably didn't want to.

It was silly the way her eyes stung with unshed tears. She had no right to feel hurt. It wasn't like she and Leo were even a thing.

But she wanted to be.

There. She admitted it. Dammit.

Clenching her jaw, she forced her emotions back down and slammed the hammer into the tile wall. Again. And yet again. Chunk after chunk dropped into the tub as she imagined the tile as her stupidity and tried to smash the sucker away with her hammer.

"You're not going to hit your thumb again, are you?"

Gasping at the sound of Leo's sexy tone behind her, Kaydee fumbled with her hold on the hammer, barely managing not to drop it as she twisted around to face him. "Holy... You scared the devil out of me."

"That's a shame." A crooked smile tugged his lips. "I like a woman with a devilish streak."

He was here, setting a bucket on her bathroom floor... and he was flirting with her. The invisible vise squeezing her chest disappeared. And just like that, all was right with her world again.

Adopting his grin, she placed a hand on her hip and tipped her head. "Good to know."

They smiled at each other for a few beats, and the temperature in the room rose several more degrees.

Probably, she should follow those words with action. A devilish woman would, but since Kaydee had no clue what constituted devilish, she stuck to something familiar. Manners. "Did you eat yet? Are you hungry? Thirsty?"

"I'm good," he said. "I ate before I left the ranch."

She nodded. "I...uh, didn't think you were going to make it tonight."

His playful expression turned serious. "I told you I'd help you with this, and I'm going to keep my word."

"But I feel bad," she said. "You look like you could use a break."

He shook his head. "Nah. It was just a long day at work. Long week, actually."

That last part didn't sound good. She frowned. "But it's only half over."

"Tell me about it." He scoffed.

Yep. Something was definitely wrong. "Want to talk about it?"

"Nothing to talk about, really." He bent down to retrieve a hammer and safety glasses from the bucket. "I screwed things up on Monday. And because I wasn't clear enough, my crew took down the wrong wall."

Monday?

Kaydee couldn't help but feel it was somehow her fault. "I'm sorry."

If he hadn't met her for lunch…

"Don't be." He straightened and put on the glasses. "I came up with an alternate plan that the homeowners loved, and when I told Stone about it, he told me to shake it off. He had a few issues like that when he first started, too."

He mentioned his former Ranger buddies from time to time. This Stone, and another one named Vince, came up more often. She could only imagine the bonds they formed in and out of battle. Her father and grandfather still kept in contact with their war buddies.

"He sounds like a good guy."

"He is." Some of the tightness disappeared from around Leo's mouth.

"And he's right, you know," she said. "Everyone makes mistakes. It's part of life. You'll no doubt make more. But that's okay. Nobody's perfect."

His chin lifted. "Sounds like you're speaking from experience."

"Man." She snickered. "The things I did when I first started out? This one time, I dyed a lady's hair pink…but she asked for green. The darn containers were next to each other, and I was in a hurry and grabbed the wrong one. Then this other time, I shaved a strip up the back of a baseball player's head when he sneezed."

Leo laughed. "I would've loved to have seen that."

"It's funny now, but at the time I was more horrified than he was." She shook her head as the memory came flooding back. "But with his permission, I turned it into his jersey number, and his teammates liked it so much, they had me shave their numbers on their heads, too. So don't be too hard on yourself. Like I said, nobody's perfect."

"I'm not so sure about that." He stared at her with admiration warming his gaze.

"You, Leo Reed, are way too sweet and equally distracting," she said with a smile.

"I'm not so sure about that," he repeated.

She laughed. "Well, I am, and I'm also sure this tile isn't going to remove itself." She stepped to the back of the tub and motioned for him to join her. "So come on. Let's work on this wall. I found it therapeutic…before someone scared the bejesus out of me."

He chuckled, and his expression brightened as he stepped in next to her. "Sorry about that. I did knock on your front door. I even hollered up the stairs, but I'm not surprised you didn't hear me the way you were attacking the wall."

She laughed. "Smashing tile is a great way to expend energy."

His lopsided grin returned. "I can think of a few other suggestions."

Her internal temperature passed hot and shot straight to inferno. And his nearness only increased the heat. "Me, too," she managed to say in a tone a little breathless to her ears.

"Yeah?" His smile widened, and a wicked gleam entered his eyes. "I'd love to hear them."

Chapter Seven

Kaydee's heart raced so fast she swore it was about to take flight. He was flirting with her again. Something she sucked at, but dammit, she was determined to give him something to chew on.

"I bet you would," she finally said, then turned her attention to the wall and whacked it with her hammer.

The sound of shards hitting the tub muffled his chuckle. Feeling energized and strangely content, she spent the next half hour busting out tile next to him. When Leo finished his side first, he began to load the debris into the bucket and carry it downstairs. To where? She had no idea, but by the time she finished her side, he had most of the tub cleared.

"You did great." A smile tugged his lips as he walked closer. "Sure you never did this before?"

Taking the hand he offered, she stepped out of the tub and waved her hammer between them. "I think the evidence speaks for itself."

She wore dust and debris like an accessory. He did not.

Still holding her hand, he put the empty bucket down and

slowly appraised her body. "Yes, it certainly does."

Awareness shot down to her toes and bounced back up, perking her nipples in the process. A fact that didn't escape his notice.

He removed the hammer from her hand and dropped it on the floor, along with her safety glasses. "You're hot as hell." His husky tone increased the heat pooling low in her belly.

"You think I'm hot?"

"Hell yeah." He tugged her into his arms as his mouth took hers in a deep, thorough kiss that had her melting against him.

The feel of his lean muscles, combined with his wicked tongue sweeping inside her mouth, increased her need to touch more of him. So she did, sliding her hands down his torso to slip under his shirt and stroke his hard abs. She loved how they quivered under her touch, and the low, sexy sound she ripped from his throat.

A second later, he backed her against the wall, and the kiss got out of hand real fast. Tasting and plundering, he drove her insane, and she eagerly rubbed her nipples against his chest.

Damn, that felt good. *He* felt good. So hot, and hard, and strong.

He must've enjoyed it, too, because he slid a hand up her side until his palm cupped her breast. Then his thumb brushed over her nipple, and she moaned and pressed into his touch.

Without breaking the kiss, he lifted her up and set her on the vanity, then grunted his approval when she wrapped her legs around his hips and drew him in tight. *Damn.* He was hard. Everywhere.

So hard.

Kaydee couldn't stop herself from rocking against the

bulge in his crotch. Twice.

Ripping his mouth from hers, he pushed her shirt up and tugged her bra aside. "So beautiful," he murmured before drawing a nipple into his mouth.

She moaned and rocked against him again. He was driving her mad, making her tremble, making her need... everything. With his name falling from her lips, she shoved her hands into his hair and held his head while he flicked her stiff peak with his tongue. Breath hitched in her throat.

Damn, he was good.

Still holding his head, she drew his mouth back to hers and slipped her tongue past his lips, trying to convey all the need burning her up inside.

Leo stiffened, then released her and stepped back. "Sorry," he said between ragged breaths. "I didn't mean to let things go so far."

With her entire body clamoring for more of the *things went so far*, she sucked air into her lungs. But before she could tell him she was more than happy where things where headed, she heard her front door open with a familiar knock.

"Kaydee? Leo?" her grandfather called from downstairs.

Shoot. She fixed her clothes with jerky movements.

"We're up here, removing tile," Leo replied, stepping between her and the doorway as if to block her from her grandfather's view.

He was sweet, but it wasn't necessary. Her grandfather wouldn't bother with the stairs.

She placed a hand on his shoulder and smiled at him. "Is that what they call it these days?"

His lips twitched.

"That explains why no one answered their phones," her grandfather said. "Ava sent me over to see if you two wanted any dessert."

"Yeah. Definitely," she answered her grandfather while

holding Leo's gaze.

She wanted more of his brand of dessert, too. The one he'd halted. But since that moment had passed, she'd have to settle for the food kind. Thankfully, Ava's baking was as remarkable as the woman.

Her neighbor's equally remarkable grandson motioned for Kaydee to precede him out the door. It wasn't hard to see that the apple hadn't fallen far from the tree.

Now, if only she could see why he'd stopped their embrace.

• • •

Thanks to Kaydee's confidence in him, Leo decided not to step down from his supervisor role that week. In her own nonjudgmental way, she made him realize he was putting too much pressure on himself to be perfect. And she was right. No one was, not even Stone. And his buddy certainly didn't expect Leo to be.

He owed the guys everything but was done being coddled. He hadn't been a quitter before everything went to shit overseas, and it was time they started counting on him again. Time he gave them a reason to treat him like they had before he was shot and their Ranger buddy Drew was killed.

Every night, when he closed his eyes, he saw his buddy and the little girl who died nearby that day, right down to the last detail. At first, those images and survivor's guilt had tormented him until he tried to silence the images with the pain meds for his wounds and a constant flow of alcohol. But they only served to make him do stupid things, and the images remained.

It wasn't until he realized the stress and unnecessary worry he was causing his family and friends that he finally wised the hell up and sought the professional help he desperately needed. Now, after fifteen months of hard work, he was in a much better place in his life…and in his head. He still saw those images every night, because he deliberately brought them to mind. It was his doing. An act of respect, to pay homage and remind himself to live and enjoy life. Something they could no longer do.

So why was he holding back with Kaydee? That was the opposite of living. That was playing it safe.

It was time to put himself out there. To experience life again.

A wave of determination washed over him. It was time to let go. To do more than flirt and steal a few kisses. Time to drop all of his guard and let whatever was going to happen… happen.

"Well now, you look like you just made a decision about something important," Brick said, walking into the tool barn. The guy carried a tile cutter in one hand as if the damn thing weighed a feather. "And I don't think it has anything to do with where you're going to put that jigsaw."

Leo glanced down at the saw in his hand. Unlike the tool belts and tools they each kept in their trucks, the bigger tools had their own barn for storage and a log to track movement should an emergency arise and a tool be needed in a hurry.

He chuckled. "But it *is* a tough decision." He placed the saw down on a shelf, then checked it in on the log.

"Right. Sure it is." Brick scratched the bridge of his nose with the thumb of his free hand, a smile tugging at his lips. "Ranks right up there with picking out china patterns and table gunners or runners or whatever the hell they're called."

Leo grinned. "Ah…Beth has you helping her fill out your registry."

The wedding was two months away, and no doubt, the most important one of the woman's career as an event planner.

"Yeah, but she's putting extra pressure on herself," Brick

said. "Worried it won't look good for business if she can't coordinate her own perfect wedding. That's why I'm not sure I should be helping. Hell, I'm the last person who knows a Hedgewood from Crouquett—"

Leo was pretty sure those names weren't correct, but it was fruitless to point it out to the clueless man.

"—or cares if lemon goes with periwinkle," Brick continued. "I just want her to be happy."

"My guess is that you helping her pick things out for your house makes her happy," Leo said.

His buddy put the tile cutter down in the corner with a sigh. "Yeah. Exactly. I'm hoping to end the torture tonight. We're finally on the last damn page."

"So I take it you're not staying for the group session?"

Brick looked up from the logbook and shook his head. "Nah. Gonna get this registry nailed down tonight if it's the last thing I do. What about you?"

"Can't make it tonight." As it was, Leo had just enough time to grab a quick shower and get to Dallas around the time Kaydee should return from dropping her grandfather and his grandmother off at bingo.

His buddy fell into step as they walked toward the door. "Heading up to Dallas to see your grandmother?"

"Yeah." He locked the barn but didn't bother to enlighten the man about Kaydee.

There wasn't time. Not if he wanted to beat the traffic and spend an hour or two with her. Alone. Which he did.

So he showered, changed, and rushed north, holding a piece of barbecue chicken Vince shoved in his hand on the way out the door. By the time he pulled into his grandmother's driveway, the chicken was gone and Kaydee was home.

Instead of going into his grandmother's house, he strode across the street and knocked on Kaydee's door. The fleeting urge to run, to play it safe and steer them back into the friend zone, flickered through him. But as soon as the door opened and her warm, welcoming smile met his, he relaxed, wanting to do more than exist, wanting to feel again. And damn, Kaydee sure as hell made him feel.

"Hi." She stood back to let him in, her voice a little breathless, as if maybe he made her feel, too. "You made good time."

Holding her gaze, he stepped inside and grinned. "I was motivated."

"You were?" Her eyes rounded, and a pretty blush colored her cheeks.

Damn, she was beautiful.

"Yep."

She cleared her throat, but the grin remained, while she waved at the boxes stacked near the stairs. "I wasn't aware that hanging tile could be fun."

"Oh, it can be. Trust me."

"I'm…ah…not sure we're talking about the same thing," she said. "So I'll take your word for it."

They stood there smiling at each other, and he knew if he didn't move, the tile wouldn't make it upstairs tonight.

He stepped past her and grabbed a box. "I didn't think you'd have trouble finding it in stock."

On Wednesday, he'd figured out how much of the standard white subway tile she'd need for her shower so she could buy it and have it ready for him to install this weekend. Thankfully, she'd listened and hadn't tried to carry the tile upstairs herself.

"They had plenty."

After placing the last box in the bathroom, he turned around to find she'd followed him upstairs and was smiling at him in the doorway.

"What?"

"Those boxes were damn heavy, and you haven't even

broken a sweat."

Oh, he was hot all right, but not from lifting tile. The way desire deepened the brown in her eyes was making him even hotter.

He stepped toward her. "Why do I get the feeling you're thinking of something else now?"

"Because I am." Her grin widened. "The guy at the store told me my taste in tile was common, and I can't help but think about how your *taste* is anything but common."

Shit.

He inhaled as awareness spiked through his body. "Kaydee...damn...you shouldn't say things like that."

"Why not?" She smiled. "It's true."

That did nothing to lessen the need rushing through him. "You're making it hard for me to concentrate on working. The tile—"

"Can wait," she said, cutting him off, more color infusing her cheeks. "I mean, if you want."

Jesus.

"Oh, I want," he said, brushing her heated cheek with the back of his knuckles. As much as he wanted to take things further, he needed to be certain she understood the risk. "I want very much, but are you sure, Kaydee? You're my grandmother's neighbor, and your grandfather is...seeing my grandmother or something. I just don't want to make anything awkward for you."

She ran her hands up his chest and shifted closer. "I appreciate it, but I'm done fighting this crazy attraction between us. So if you're done fighting it, too, then yeah, I'm very sure."

Chapter Eight

Her words and the feel of her soft curves barely brushing his body washed away the last of Leo's caution. With his heart beating hard in his chest, he cupped her face in both hands and kissed her without holding back.

Being with Kaydee may turn out to be a mistake. A damn big one, but right now, at this moment, Leo didn't care. Everything faded away when he touched her.

The weight on his shoulders.

Guilt.

Shame.

Worry.

It all disappeared in her arms. And heaven help him, it was damned addicting. And although they'd only kissed and touched a few times, each embrace was incredibly better than the last.

Tonight was proving no exception.

The beautiful woman's reactions to his kisses and touches made him starve for more. So much so, he was barely holding it together as he crushed her closer.

A soft moan rumbled in her throat, and she pressed him against the door, then rubbed her sweet curves up and down his body.

Son of a bitch…she felt good.

"Leo," she uttered when they broke for air, her fingers fisting his hair before pulling his mouth so close her lips brushed his as she spoke. "I want you so bad I can taste it." Then she kissed him, again and again, moaning into his mouth as if he were the best thing she ever tasted.

Holy shit, the woman had him hard and throbbing like no other.

With need calling the shots, he bent and swept her off her feet, uncaring that her flip-flops fell off when he carried her into the hall. "Which is your room?"

"Last door on the left," she replied near his ear before sinking her teeth in his neck.

Son of a…

Reaching the room, he set her feet down and immediately pressed her against the nearest wall, where he captured her wicked mouth. She moaned again and wrapped her leg around his thigh, tugging him closer.

Damn woman was trying to kill him.

After he entwined their fingers and held her hands against the wall on either side of her head, he slowed the kiss, brushing his tongue just inside her bottom lip. She let out another of her sexy little sounds and squeezed his hands.

Taking that to mean she wanted more, he swept his tongue fully inside her hot mouth and slowly, thoroughly explored every delicious inch. She tugged her hands free to shove them under his shirt while her tongue brushed his, upping his already-erratic pulse.

Her responses were amazing, and he noted she was far from alone. His stomach quivered where she stroked, and he was still wrapping his brain around that when she broke the kiss to push his shirt up.

Always happy to lend a hand, he stepped back and yanked it over his head, then stopped breathing when she inhaled and stared at him with a crazed hunger heating her gaze.

"Jesus, Kaydee, if you don't stop looking at me like that I'm going to burst."

"Don't do that." She shook her head and stepped past him. "Not yet."

He twisted around and was about to respond when she turned to face him, grasped the bottom of her tank top and ripped it over her head, presenting him a mouthwatering view of generous curves spilling out of a lacy white bra.

"Damn," he breathed, heart rocking in his chest when she popped the hook on her bra, and two seconds later, stood before him in nothing but her cutoffs.

Then she unfastened her shorts and they fell to her feet, leaving her in a sexy scrap of white lace.

Leo almost swallowed his tongue. Almost. But he had plans for it and her. He stepped right up to those soft, supple curves and tugged her against him. She was too damn gorgeous for him to keep his distance any longer. Capturing her startled gasp with his mouth, he gave in to the hunger only Kaydee inspired.

And he was inspired. So damn much.

After several glorious moments, he released her lips to drag in air while he kissed a path to the curve of her neck.

"Damn...Leo." She gasped again and raked her fingernails across his back. "Your jaw..."

He stilled and drew back, frowning at her reddening skin. "Christ, Kaydee. I'm sorry."

"What? Why?" She blinked. "No. Don't be. It feels amazing. Please don't stop."

Relief washed through him. He hated the thought of

hurting her.

She reached for him and grinned—a wicked grin that wrecked his pulse while her hand slowly trailed down his body to strum his abs and brush the waistband of his jeans. "You have more clothes on than I do. We should rectify that."

He captured her wrist and brought her bold hand to his lips. "Oh, we're going to rectify a lot of things."

Her grin broadened, and she ran her free hand down his chest and abs again. "Good to know," she said in a low, breathless tone, then traced his erection through his jeans. "I hope freeing you is one of them, because damn, I'm so ready."

Ah hell. She was definitely trying to kill him.

"Sit on the bed," he said in a rough voice.

Heaven help him, her eyes flared with the same fierce need rushing through him as he stalked her the whole way. The instant the back of her knees hit the mattress, she sat down, and her gorgeous breasts bounced, beckoning his attention. He gave it willingly, dropping to his knees to cup each one, delighting in the way her nipples puckered under his touch.

The woman was absolutely breathtaking.

"*Leo.*" Her deep, throaty tone and the way she arched into his hands had blood whistling through his ears and a shaft of heat shooting straight to his throbbing groin.

Fierce hunger ruled his thoughts and actions, sharpening his focus to just the two of them. All that mattered was pleasing Kaydee and giving in to the heat consuming them.

Leaning forward, he sucked a delicious peak into his mouth and rolled the other between his thumb and forefinger, tugging both until she moaned and arched her body again. Wanting to up her pleasure, he removed his mouth from her nipple and blew on her wet skin, smiling at her hiss of breath. He switched sides, needing to hear her sexy sounds some more.

Leo pressed her back to the mattress, then brushed his lips over her ribs and belly to nip at her hips. He wanted to lick and bite and taste every inch of her gorgeous body. And would. Later. Right now, his mission concerned the paradise waiting for him beneath her lace. He hooked his fingers under the sexy material and tugged it off, then kneeling in front of her, he placed a hand on each leg and spread her wide.

Every last part of him tightened while his mouth watered, longing to taste the exquisiteness before him.

"Leo…" Her plea was full of need. "Are you going to stare or do any of that rectifying you spoke about?"

He grinned. "Both." Holding her gaze, he ran a hand up her trembling thigh to lightly stroke her glistening folds.

She jumped and sucked in a breath.

"Definitely both." He placed her legs over his shoulders and tugged her sweet ass to the edge of the bed. "And taste, too," he said before leaning down to put his mouth on her.

Another of her throaty sounds met his ears while her hands went to his head. The more he experimented and explored, the tighter her fingers dug into his scalp. He didn't care. He reveled in her reactions, and continued until he discovered the rhythm and length of stroke that did her in. It stuck in his memory, as did the sight of her, the sound and taste of her.

She rocked her hips. "Damn…your beard…it feels amazing."

Beard? He didn't have one. Not really. Not a full one, although he hadn't shaved in over a week.

Her head lifted off the mattress, and she met his gaze. "So amazing."

What was amazing was her taste. But he didn't tell her. That would require him to remove his mouth from her sweetness, which wasn't happening. Not until she was thoroughly satisfied.

After making several more passes with his tongue, he curled it and dipped inside, upping his pace. Kaydee's hold increased, and she moaned his name as she arched off the bed.

Blood pounded through his ears, and his heart nearly burst from his chest. She could make him bald for all he cared. He'd never felt so alive.

But as much as he loved holding her on the brink, he knew he hovered much too close to the edge himself. He was reaching it. Fast. But it wasn't time for him. Not yet.

Drawing back, he blew on her wet flesh in short concentrated bursts.

"Leo..."

Sliding a finger inside her, he leaned forward to gently take her back into his mouth. That sent her over. Kaydee burst and cried out his name in a breathy, erotic tone forever burned in his head.

No one had ever said his name like that.

Damn...it was exhilarating.

He brought her down slowly, barely hanging on to his control. She was so much better than he'd imagined. And he needed to be inside her, because that would no doubt be better than he'd imagined, too.

Drawing back, he put her legs down, then shot to his feet to quickly shed the rest of his clothes. The beauty watched him fish a condom from his jeans and roll it on. Her face was flushed, and her expression was satiated. Warmth spread through his chest. *He* put that satisfied look on her face.

She lifted up on her elbows and smiled at him. "That was...you were...wow."

He liked "wow," and the fact that she had trouble talking.

A wicked gleam entered her eyes. "Now it's time we take care of you."

Chapter Nine

Kaydee scooted up the mattress and spread her legs.

Leo's heart stopped for a full beat, then nearly rocked out of his damn chest. How the hell had he gotten so lucky? Because, yeah...hell, yeah. That was exactly where he wanted to be.

Without hesitation, he crawled over her, bending down to kiss a path up her soft curves, paying special attention to her sensitive nipples on his way to her neck. She sighed and ran her hands down his back, then clutched him as he guided his fingers between her legs. *So wet.* He swallowed. Hard. And clenched his jaw in an attempt to keep his cool.

"So good." She rocked into his strokes. "How can you have me ready so soon? But I am, Leo. I need you inside me."

Ah hell. He was done. Straightening, he positioned his tip at her slick entrance, grabbed her hips, and pushed slowly inside.

So damn perfect.

He *knew* she'd feel perfect.

"Oh...wow." Her voice was but a whisper.

He clenched his jaw, fighting the urge to drive the rest of the way in. "You okay? Still with me?"

"Yes. All the way," she said on a hitched breath, and proved it by lifting her hips until she took in every fucking inch.

Damn. That felt good. She felt good. So damn fucking good.

For the first time in over two years—no...*ever*—Leo was in heaven. He felt amazing. At peace. Just...good.

He felt good.

It'd been so long. He'd nearly forgotten how wonderful *good* felt.

"I'm with you, Leo," she murmured. "*So* with you, but I need you to move."

He choked out a laugh. He needed that, too. "Your fault," he said. "You feel..."

"Rectified?" she teased.

God, she had this amazing way of making him smile, too.

"Working on it." He dipped down to kiss her quick before pressing his palms on the mattress on either side of her head and locking his elbows. "I'm working on it," he repeated, holding her gaze as he began to thrust.

Slow, at first, wanting to enjoy the feel of her warmth engulfing him. The drag and pull of their bodies was already nearly too much. Hunger and tenderness washed through him. He could take her hard and fast, or slower and savor the bliss.

He aimed for something in between.

Leaning down, he captured one of her beckoning nipples in his mouth, while he lifted enough to slide a hand between them to stroke the spot that drove her wild.

"Leo...I..." Kaydee moaned beneath him, trembling and bucking and tightening around him while she burst.

He watched her face as she went over the edge. Her eyes

closed, she threw her head back, and her lips parted with a moan that nearly took him with her.

Damn, that was hot.

He was going to hold on to that image forever. It was honest, and pure, and real. As real as the heat spiraling down his back and tingling his balls. He straightened and grasped her hips, pulling nearly all the way out before plunging deep, calling her name as he let go of his control and came with her. As he pumped in and out, he closed his eyes, and his whole being centered on their connection and the feel of warm, slick heat hugging him tight, embracing him as she continued to coax out the fiercest release of his life.

It was wild and intense, and when he was finally spent, he collapsed on top of her, dragging air into his lungs. The woman was a thief. A beautiful, sensual, sexy thief who stole his breath. And his bones. Yeah, they were definitely gone, because he sure as shit couldn't feel any.

A few seconds later, he mustered enough strength to roll off her so she could breathe. "Still with me?"

"Yes." Panting, she turned to him and smiled. "Look forward to coming with you again."

He laughed. God, he loved her wit. "That could be arranged."

"Good to know." She turned onto her side and rested her chin in her hand. "This artwork is amazing," she said while skimming her free hand lightly over the tattoo on his arm.

"The bottom part's new." Christ. Why the hell did he tell her that?

Her finger softly traced the boots beneath the rifle. "A fallen soldier, right?"

"Yeah."

Shit.

What was wrong with him?

He never talked about his tattoo. Or the reason behind

the new part—Drew. Dammit. Great sex relaxed more than his body. It loosened his damn tongue. She literally fucked him stupid.

"I'm sorry," she said, brushing her lips over the ink.

Unexpected and fierce, a rash of emotions swirled inside his chest. Part of him wanted to run the hell away, but the other part wanted to crush her close.

Let happen whatever was going to happen…

Before driving here today, he'd made that decision. And he would, as long as he didn't have to talk about his past. That wasn't going to happen. No way. It would lead to telling her about his mistakes, and he couldn't bear to see disappointment cloud the satisfaction he'd put in her eyes. He liked how she saw him. Whole. Strong. At least that was the impression she gave him. He didn't want her opinion of him tainted by his past.

Yeah, he was done talking. But it was too early to go fetch Nate and his grandmother from the rec center.

Kaydee suddenly sat up and inhaled. "Oh my gosh. I'm sorry, Leo. You must be starving. I didn't offer you any supper."

"It's okay. Vince shoved a piece of chicken in my hand on the way out the door, and I ate it while I drove here." He smiled and sat up, too. "And you most certainly did offer me supper." Reaching out, he glided his finger up her ribs, over the swell of her breast to one deliciously puckering tip. "Seems my appetite for what you offered has suddenly returned."

• • •

By the time Sunday afternoon rolled around, the tile was finished…and so was Kaydee. Almost. This would be her fourth time that weekend. Or was it the fifth? She'd lost count, thanks to the incredible man—naked in all his splendor—

rolling a condom on in the middle of her living room. What had started out with Leo helping her spackle a few holes somehow ended up with the front door locked and the two of them naked.

Damn, he was gorgeous. Magnificent, even. All long, lean planes and hard muscle. That sexy tattoo and the way his muscles rippled underneath. The thought of licking, and nipping, and tasting every single delicious inch of him made her heart flutter in her chest.

This thing between them was crazy and surprisingly strong, and she had no idea how long it would last, *if* she wanted it to last, or even if *he* wanted it to last. Opening up, letting someone in, wasn't something that came easy to Kaydee, and yet she already knew she'd miss Leo if things didn't work out. Or when she left. Because she eventually would. That restlessness was sure to be overwhelming by the time her dad retired and her parents moved here to free her up to leave.

She'd miss Leo's wit, and his smile, and that square jaw of his, with the perpetual scruff her whole body had the immense pleasure of experiencing more than once. Looking at him made her feel good. Being with him made her feel good. Hell, *he* made her feel good.

Eyeing his well-defined chest, and how the muscles at his hips cut to form a vee, she tried not to drool. Yeah, she'd miss all that, too. Very much. And the mind-blowing orgasms so intense they zapped her strength.

"Now, where were we?" He stepped in front of her, but instead of crushing her close as she half expected, he ran his hands lightly up her arms, then down her back, before leaning in to gently sink his teeth into her earlobe.

She sucked in a breath and gripped his shoulder blades. "Right about there." Tipping her head to give him more access, she closed her eyes and sighed. He knew how to rev her up…how to get her going. He was magic. His tongue flicked her earlobe before his lips slid down her throat to the curve of her neck, and the slow burn in her belly spread south. "Mmm…" He smelled of spackling and soap and heat, and it made her mad with longing. "Leo…"

"I know," he said, as if feeling the same craziness. A heartbeat later, he kissed her, a light, openmouthed connection that made her gasp as the tip of his tongue traced her lips. But then he pulled back, and watching her, gaze hot, he smiled.

She glanced at his lips, wanting them back on hers so badly she could taste it. He complied with a soft, brief kiss. Then another. And still another. Bugger was teasing her. "*Leo.*"

"Right here." He shoved his hands in her hair and finally took her mouth.

It was an amazing kiss. Absolutely perfect. Hot and decadent, with the right amount of tongue to quicken her pulse and make her quiver for more. The guy knew what he was doing. She didn't. Not when it came to him. To them. Oh, she knew the process. She enjoyed sex, but somehow, he'd taken it beyond physical, beyond simple gratification, and made her feel him emotionally. She didn't know that was possible. Never knew something like that existed. But underneath this unexpected overabundance of feeling—and God, Leo certainly made her feel good—she also felt a little lost, and more than a little panicky.

"You feel so damn good," he murmured after breaking the kiss. "It's crazy. You make me feel good, too." He ran his deliciously calloused hands down her body, and goose bumps spread across her skin in silent applause.

Her heart cracked open a little, and warmth spread through her chest. His words quieted her misgivings and empowered her. "I feel the same," she said, and needing more of his kisses, she brought his mouth back down on hers and tugged him with her as she stepped backward toward the wall.

And tripped over her discarded clothes.

Kaydee gasped and would've fallen if Leo hadn't held on to her, but that interfered with his balance, and they both stumbled until his palm hit the wall, followed by the arm he'd quickly wrapped around her.

"Oh my God. I'm sorry. Are you okay?" she asked, trying to straighten.

"I'm fine." After righting them, he planted his hands on the wall on either side of her head and looked her over. "You?"

Nodding, she blew out a breath, and a rush of heat flushed her face. "But I think I bruised my sexiness."

A gleam—wicked and deliciously hot—entered his eyes. "Not a chance." As if to prove it, he removed his hands from the wall and skimmed them over her shoulders and down her breasts. Her nipples immediately puckered. "That's damn sexy," he murmured, his breath warm on her neck as he bent to place openmouthed kisses across her shoulders, all while his thumbs brushed her nipples back and forth, reigniting her need.

Closing her eyes, she moaned and leaned back. Hard. Too hard. She *thunked* her head...

A knock sounded on the wall behind her. The wall she shared with her grandfather.

Kaydee and Leo both stilled.

"Everything okay?" her grandfather's muffled voice came through the wall.

She met Leo's gaze. "Yeah," she replied, but her own voice was too throaty. She cleared the rasp away and tried again. "Yes. We're working on the wall. Everything's fine—"

Leo grinned, a sexy, decadent grin, and dipped down to kiss her breast before sucking the tip into his mouth hard.

"Oh...yeah..." She closed her eyes. That felt amazing. Her whole body trembled.

"Want help?" her grandfather asked.

No!

She opened her eyes. "Th-thanks, but we're good."

So good. Damn, Leo had a talented mouth. He switched to her other breast, kissing and licking until he closed his teeth gently over her nipple.

"Well, holler if you need me," her grandfather said.

Air funneled into her throat. "'Kay." Hopefully he heard, because there was no way she could say any more now.

Good glory, Leo knew his way around a woman's body. She wanted to move and moan and switch places but was too conscious of her grandfather just on the other side.

"Let's move," she whispered down to Leo.

Lifting his head, he flashed her a grin, and in the blink of an eye, he had her resting against her credenza on the opposite wall. "Better?" he asked, but didn't wait for an answer. Instead, he dropped to his knees and placed his mouth back on her body.

"Much," she managed as he kissed his way to her belly.

Kaydee stared down her torso at him, watching his hands slide to her inner thighs. They were tan and big and masterful.

Glancing up, he held her gaze while he nudged her legs apart with his shoulders, then he dropped his gaze to stare at her goods. "Damn, you make my mouth water." He brushed his thumbs upward, and they grazed her center.

She sucked in air, grateful to have the credenza behind her.

"Hold on to me," he said, moving his thumbs again. And then again, and this time he leaned in and placed his mouth on her, too.

Her knees shook. She grasped his shoulders and closed her eyes, giving in to the sensations racking her body. He was driving her crazy. So crazy.

Apparently on a mission to zap every single last one of

her brain cells, Leo added his tongue to the task, licking up and down, and back up…

Tightening her hold, she arched into him and moaned. She knew she should be quiet. Her grandfather might still hear, but her body seemed to be on a mission, too. A mission to let Leo know just how amazing he was making her feel.

With his mouth still trying to drive away her sanity, he slid a finger inside her. Again. And yet again. Unable to keep quiet or hold on to her control, she cried out in a low, throaty sound as he drove her right over the edge. She rocked into him and shuddered wildly as she came. Standing.

Definitely masterful.

By the time she came back to herself, she was leaning heavily against the side of the credenza, and he was smiling a smug, smoldering smile.

"Catch the number of the bus that just wrecked me?" she asked.

He chuckled and stepped close. "I'm not done," he said, bringing her hand to his impressive erection. "This is—" The amusement seemed to back up in his throat on a sharp inhale when she stroked him long and slow. "Damn, Kaydee," he groaned.

She hopped up onto the credenza and shook her head. "Shh…I'm not done," she mocked him, then reached out to gently guide him home.

He needed no further instruction. Taking over, he pushed inside her, a delicious, warm slide, and she had one last thought before the last of her brain function disappeared under a tsunami of sensual fog.

If opening her heart and letting this man get close meant he'd stay in her life a little longer, then she was damn sure going to take that chance. She just hoped it wouldn't come back to bite her in the ass.

Chapter Ten

Later that evening, Kaydee was in her living room, chilling with Fiona for their Sunday Netflix binge-watching ritual. Tonight, they were starting the second season of *Daredevil*, but her mind was on another superhero and the knack he had for making her feel super, too.

It was a new feeling. One she was willing to entertain for a long time. That was new, too. She wasn't the "long for more" type. A fruitless sentiment. One that—she discovered in the past—didn't bode well for her restless spirit.

"So…" Fiona sat at the other end of the couch and grinned. "You and Leo were busy, I see." She paused meaningfully. "Doing…like, say…each other."

Kaydee's gaze immediately shot to the credenza, looking for signs of their amazing sexcapade from earlier that afternoon. Thankfully, she found none. She turned to her friend and frowned. "What do you mean?"

Fi snorted. "Oh, come on, Kay. You answered the door with a satisfied grin on your face, and it hasn't wavered one bit. Only really great sex could cause that phenomenon."

She pointed to the spackled wall. "We worked on my house."

"And each other." Amusement lit her friend's gaze. "Don't bother to deny it. I ran into Leo at the gas station earlier, and he was wearing an identical 'just-got-lucky' grin."

"He was?" Warmth spread through Kaydee, and she felt her whole body soften.

"It's about time you two stepped off the friend bus and acted on your attraction." Fi touched her arm. "I'm happy for you."

Since she was obviously busted, Kaydee didn't deny it. "Thanks. I am happy. Happier than I can honestly say I've ever been." She inhaled and decided to be completely truthful. "And that scares me to death."

"Why?" Her friend frowned. "It's a good thing."

"Not if it suddenly goes away." She'd been through that so many times growing up. Too many. She was the queen of investing in relationships, then moving. Starting all over. Then moving again. After the fourth time, she simply stopped investing. But she hadn't stopped moving around, even after striking out on her own. Settling in one place was *un*settling. It made her feel claustrophobic. The need for constant change was an itch she wasn't sure she'd ever shake.

Fi lifted a shoulder. "That's why it's called taking a chance. Sometimes it doesn't work out, but sometimes it does and it's totally worth it."

Kaydee knew that, too. At least, with her friend. They met at the technical college in the beauty education track. That first day, she'd expected to form another fleeting friendship, but Fiona was different. They clicked, and Kaydee realized she didn't want it to end. So by the time graduation came around, she had plans with Fi to get a job in the same salon.

"I really hope you won't run from your feelings," Fiona was saying. "You've done it your whole life. Let go of that tight control of yours and just enjoy yourself for a change."

Exactly what she had in mind.

The smiling woman dipped her head to catch Kaydee's attention. "If Leo can put that dreamy look in your eyes, then, hun, I think he's worth taking a chance. Enjoy it."

She returned the smile. "Oh, trust me. I have every intention of enjoying Leo."

Many times.

• • •

At the end of the week, Leo and Stone, Brick, Vince, and Cord found themselves in one of those rare instances where they all finished early on a Friday. Taking advantage of the unexpected situation, they decided to kick back in the ranch rec room, crack open a beer, and shoot some pool.

"To Leo," Stone said, holding up his bottle, and everyone followed suit. "Congratulations on completing your toughest job. Supervising *your* first crew...solo."

The end of the workweek also brought with it the end of Leo's first supervising job. Ultimately, he was pleased with the outcome, and—more importantly—so were the clients. The Burmans had signed off an hour ago, and Leo had sent his crew home.

"It didn't go without a hitch," he felt compelled to point out, before taking a swig.

Vince snorted. "What job does?"

Brick nodded and tipped back his beer.

Cord chalked his cue. "Were the clients pleased?"

"Yeah," he said. Mrs. Burman hadn't stopped smiling or gushing about the extra openness of her kitchen thanks to their altered plan. "They already left a review online." A positive one. He checked.

He took a deep breath, his lungs expanding to their

fullest, and he stood straighter. All and all, good feelings abounded. Same could be said for things with Kaydee. A smile tugged his lips. He felt right when he was inside her.

"So, Leo." Vince leaned on his stick while Stone started the game.

The crack of pool balls echoed through the room. It was the Mitchum brothers versus Vince and Cord. Leo was sitting this game out.

He raised a brow. "What?"

"You've been walking around with that smile on your face all week. When are you going to tell us her name?"

Shit.

Stone shot Vince a glare. "Don't mind him. It's just great to see you smile."

Cord locked his superpower Warlock stare on him for a beat, then dipped his head once. "Definitely a girl."

"For sure," Brick said.

Stone grinned. "She lives near his grandmother."

"And you know that how?" Brick asked.

Leo stood there and drank his beer, watching the exchange, content to keep quiet.

"Because I listen with my ears. You should try it sometime." Stone lined up another shot, but his grin never wavered.

"Hey," Brick snapped. "I listen."

Vince rolled his eyes. "Yeah, with your stomach. Beth told me."

A grin spread across the older Mitchum's face. "True."

Leo laughed. His buddies were a bunch of assholes. But they were his assholes. And he was lucky as hell to call them friends.

It was Cord's turn, because Stone missed the pocket. He studied the balls on the table. "She must be special."

"Yeah." Brick lifted his bottle but didn't drink. "She

have a name?"

Vince snorted. "Of course she has a name. Everyone does, you doofus."

"It's Kaydee," Leo finally said. "She lives across the street from my grandmother in one side of a duplex, and her grandfather lives in the other. She did it so she can keep an eye on him, while he still has privacy."

"That's very admirable," Cord said.

"And smart." Brick stepped up to the table and shot the cue ball into a red ball, but it hit just shy of a pocket.

Leo frowned. He wasn't sure that was a compliment. "Smart? What do you mean?"

Brick moved away from the table to let Vince shoot. "*She* has her privacy, too." A big-ass grin spread across the goof's face. "As I'm sure you've no doubt realized."

He chuckled. "Yep. You're an idiot."

"True." The smiling fool reached for the beer he'd placed on the bar behind Leo. "But I'm also right. Hence that 'got my world rocked' grin plastered on your face all week."

Had he really grinned all week?

"Don't listen to my idiot brother." Stone swiped the cue from Brick and met Leo's gaze. "She sounds great. I'm happy for you."

Vince straightened from his missed shot. "Me, too. Maybe you can bring her by one of these days. Just let me know if there's a special dish she enjoys."

Bring Kaydee to At-Ease...

Normally, Leo would shoot the offer down before it had a chance to grow into an idea that everyone would insist was a good one. But he was too slow. As expected, someone did.

Him.

That simple fact made him wonder what the hell was wrong with him. Why would he even entertain the idea?

As soon as those questions flickered through his mind,

the answer to both immediately followed.

Kaydee.

She was what was wrong with him, although "wrong" in a good way. He liked Kaydee. He liked being with her, and the way she treated him like he was a good person. She had a way of making him feel…absolved. And God, that was addicting.

"I'm sure Leo will bring her around when he's ready," Stone said, sinking another ball. Even on the home front the guy always had his back.

"Stone's right." Cord replaced Brick's empty bottle with a full one. "Let's drop it."

"Leo knows we don't mean no harm, and we're actually trying to help," Brick said. "No one was more clueless than I was with Beth. Except maybe you with Haley," he said to Cord. "Man, you ignored your attraction to her for *years*."

Leo fought a grin. Yeah, both men hadn't handled things so great with their women in the beginning. But his situation with Kaydee was different. Especially since she wasn't his woman. They weren't in a long-term thing.

"Don't listen to them." Vince chuckled. "You and Kaydee just keep doing whatever it is you're doing. It looks good on you."

"Damn good." Stone grinned, watching Cord line up a shot. "You heading back up there this weekend?"

Leo nodded. "Yeah."

Instead of bingo, his grandmother wanted to go line dancing with him, Kaydee, and Nate to celebrate the end of his first job. He held back a grunt. Dancing. He hadn't danced in years. Although the thought of holding Kaydee close was a huge plus.

"What are you working on this time?" Brick asked, then wagged his brows. "Or is that a foolish question?"

"No, bro." Stone sighed. "*That* was the foolish question."

Leo laughed. It was damn good to see the humor and well-meaning in their words without anger and self-deprecation getting in the way. It'd been so long—too long—since his thoughts centered on something other than guilt and self-loathing. "I'm going to repair the stairs to her basement."

"That's good," Stone said. "And if you and Kaydee are a thing or become a thing, that's good, too. Just know it probably won't go without a glitch. That's normal. Men are assholes, so we're going to screw up. It's in our DNA."

Leo nodded, although he had no idea what made his buddy think he and Kaydee were long term. They were only light and casual. More of a fun friends-with-benefits kind of thing. Anything more would involve his past, and that would ruin her outlook toward him. He liked feeling absolved and knew he'd always feel that way when he looked back on their encounters.

He'd have to be crazy to jeopardize that.

Chapter Eleven

Kaydee loved surprises.

Leo's call earlier that day to ask if she wanted to go line dancing with him, her grandfather, and Ava, definitely qualified as one. It was both great and unexpected. Of course, it wouldn't be a surprise if it was expected.

She was glad she'd taken the time to paint her nails the same coral shade as her strapless sundress when Ava explained the reason for Leo's surprise invitation. Tonight was a special occasion. They were celebrating the conclusion of Leo's first job as a supervisor.

By the time their drinks arrived and they placed their orders for a round of burgers and fries, Kaydee was ready to go straight to dessert.

In the dimly lit honky-tonk, Leo's dark hair gleamed black and curled where it hit his shoulders, making his startling blue eyes stand out even more. Add his sexy scruff to the mix, and damn, he was smokin' hot. And that wasn't even taking into account the lean lines of his muscled body emphasized under his white button-down shirt and blue jeans that had worn creases in the right places.

When he'd shown up on her doorstep a half hour ago, she'd nearly swallowed her tongue at the sexy vision he presented. Of course, she didn't tell him. No guy wanted to hear they're a vision, but he was one. Big-time. And her heartbeat hadn't leveled off since.

"To my grandson. I'm so proud of you," Ava said, eyes turning misty as she held up a glass of beer.

"Yes." Her grandfather lifted his beer as well. "Congratulations on a job well done, son."

Opting to share a pitcher of ginger ale with Leo, Kaydee raised her glass and watched as he shifted in his seat. Poor guy seemed to be uncomfortable dealing with positive attention.

That kind of broke her heart.

She reached under the table and entwined the fingers of their free hands. "To Leo."

There was a ton more she wanted to add, but her throat swelled for some reason, so she left it at that. Besides, no matter what platitudes she spouted, she knew they'd only add to his discomfort. That was the last thing she wanted.

He raised his glass. "Thank you." And when he squeezed her hand, she met his gaze and knew his words had been meant for her.

So was the heart-stopping smile on his face. It was real, and open, and it felt like the sun was shining down on her. She returned his smile, and her entire body softened under his attention, and probably the small circles he drew on her hand with his thumb helped, too. Goose bumps were now shooting up her arm.

"You know, you kids don't have to pretend anymore," Ava said, just as Kaydee had the misfortune of taking a sip of the ginger ale.

She coughed and sputtered while glancing at the woman through blurry vision. "Pretend what?"

"That you two aren't an item," Ava replied.

"Yeah, you're busted, hun," her grandfather chimed in, big grin on his face. "It's okay."

Heat flooded her cheeks. Ah crap. Maybe he *had* heard them on Sunday...

"And about damn time you got around to asking her out, Leo," Ava continued. "It's good to see you're not ignoring the attraction anymore."

Leo squeezed her hand again, and she watched his smile return. "I agree."

"Good." Ava nodded, satisfaction warming her gaze. "Then what do you say we all get out there and hit a dance or two before our food arrives?"

"Yes, ma'am," Leo said.

Sliding his chair back, he helped Kaydee to her feet. Uncertainty skittered through his gaze. "Unless you don't want to dance?"

This time, she squeezed *his* hand. "I'd very much like to dance with you."

A big smile curved his lips, and for the next hour and a half, they danced and ate and danced some more. Kaydee was far from surprised to discover the man had moves. Lord knew he had the right ones when they were naked. Only logical he'd have them on the dance floor, too.

The last time she'd had this much fun was...never. She couldn't remember a time she'd laughed and let loose without giving it a second thought. It just happened, and she rolled with it. Hell, she was even wearing a grin when washing her hands after a restroom break. The woman staring back at her in the mirror had a flushed face, a curved mouth, and a dreamy look in her eyes.

"Looks good on you," Ava said, appearing in the reflection with her. "Leo has the same alive expression on his face. Thank you for putting it there, my dear."

She turned to face the woman and shook her head. "I didn't do anything."

Ava laughed. "Bullshit."

"But I didn't." She really hadn't done anything special. Nothing any red-blooded woman wouldn't do.

"I'm not talking about sex." Ava shook her head and waved her hands, and Kaydee was extremely relieved they were the only two in the bathroom. "He could get that anywhere."

That wiped the smile from her face.

"It's different with you. He's gotten so much more."

A slight tug returned to her lips, and with it, a burst of warmth through her chest.

"You've reached him when no one else has been able to." Her neighbor sobered and drew in a ragged breath, her gaze going misty again. "It has been a long, long time since I had my grandson back. Thank you, Kaydee." Ava pulled her in for a hug and squeezed. "Please keep doing whatever it is you're doing."

Her heart dropped to her knees. It sounded like the woman was talking about something more than a fling. A relationship. Kaydee didn't do them. But truthfully, she didn't want things with Leo to end. At least not yet. Other than sex, he didn't spout promises, or stress her out by talking about a future. They were enjoying a fun, casual here and now. She wanted to keep seeing him that way.

So she smiled and squeezed back. "I will."

"Good." Ava sighed, and when she drew back, a hint of mischief danced in her eyes. "Any chance you could occupy him until morning, instead of him sneaking into my house in the middle of the night, like he did Friday and Saturday last weekend?"

Kaydee was pretty sure there wasn't a name for the shade of red her face sported. It'd gone clear past crimson.

First, she'd learned her grandfather might've heard them on Sunday, and now she discovered his grandmother was aware that Leo had been at her place until the wee hours of the morning last weekend.

Right now would be a great time for Scotty to beam her up. Or the floor to open and swallow her. Of course, neither happened, because they weren't possible. Unlike her megablush.

"It's okay." Ava chuckled, patting her cheek. "You're both adults, old enough to know what you're doing. Same goes for your grandfather and me, although we'd like to do it all night, not have to cut things short, because Leo might return to the next room at some point."

Holy hookups…

She swallowed a laugh. Those two faced the same issues as she and Leo had—

"Last thing I want is to be in the middle of the throes when he returns." Ava continued to speak, and Kaydee's face continued to flame. "So…do you think you can keep him occupied all night?"

"Um…" She cleared her throat. "Yeah. I'd be happy to. Sure."

Crap. She stumbled over her words like an idiot, but she could hardly believe the conversation she was having.

Good Lord, she just promised her…her…what exactly was Leo? Her friend? Boyfriend? The guy she was sleeping with? Whatever he was, she'd just promised his grandmother she'd keep him in her bed until morning, so his grandmother could keep Kaydee's grandfather in bed until then, too.

Oh my God, what a night, she thought as she walked back to the table with Ava, her gaze meeting Leo's as she approached. Given his lopsided grin and the heat and amusement in his eyes, he apparently just had a similar crazy conversation with her grandfather. And he was totally on board with it, too.

Her pulse leaped. It'd been a long time since she let a man stay all night.

Perhaps that was because she hadn't been with the right man. Leo was different, and the way she felt about him was different, too. Stronger. Better. He made her happy. Made her feel like she mattered. Until that moment, Kaydee hadn't realized how much she'd needed that.

She just hoped letting him stay didn't jinx things between them.

• • •

Tonight they were actually going to sleep together—as in, fall asleep together—and not just have sex. Leo knew this, and yet when he walked into Kaydee's house later that night, and she locked the door behind him, his heart raced. Not with trepidation, but anticipation. Excitement.

Need.

He liked Kaydee. A lot. A hell of a lot. But still, this was a huge step, not just for him, but for her, too. He knew keeping things a secret from their grandparents hadn't been the only reason she'd never asked him to stay the night. Hard to keep someone at arm's length after you've fallen asleep with them. It was perhaps even more intimate than sex. A step further than casual. He was starting to suspect she had some type of commitment issue. Either from constantly being ripped from friendships at a young age and being too afraid to form an attachment, or from embracing the wanderlust lifestyle and growing restless staying in one place too long. Either way, it was a commitment issue. Hell, how could she not have one? Being an army brat was tough.

It was the reason he and the guys had made a pact, during their active-duty years, to never get seriously involved with a woman. With the exception of Drew. He'd already been married when he started Ranger training, and his death had gutted Haley. Thank God Cord had been able to help her pick up the pieces. Marriage to an active-duty soldier was a hard life, not only for the wife, but for any resulting children.

That was the last thing Leo would've needed. A child. He wasn't exactly the best father role model. Might never be. His past made sure of that.

"I had a great time tonight," Kaydee said, bringing his attention back to the present.

"Me, too," he replied, lifting a finger to lightly trace her cheek. "A really great time." Then, because he needed to taste her, suddenly needed their connection more than air, he brought his mouth down on hers, and slowly, thoroughly kissed her.

Sighing, she opened up for him and responded with a hunger that matched the one building inside him. By the time he lifted his head, they were both panting, and she was gripping his shirt, as if to keep from falling.

He liked that. A lot.

But what he didn't like was the thought of pressuring her, so he moved his hands to her shoulders—her deliciously bare shoulders—and held her gaze. "Listen, don't worry about what my grandmother asked you. I don't have to stay all night. I can go to a hotel. Just say the word."

Chapter Twelve

Kaydee's gaze softened and warmed, and the most amazing smile spread across her face. Leo felt it in his chest. What the hell? How was that even possible? It was as if his heart cracked open, and warmth—the same warmth shining in her eyes—funneled into him.

"I'd like you to stay." Honesty sweetened her tone. "That is…if you want to." She glanced down at the floor, and when her gaze returned to his, uncertainty clouded her beautiful brown eyes.

If he wanted to…

He was no longer active duty. Had a job he loved. A goal he believed in. And a woman he enjoyed spending time with. Taking this next step, investing a little bit more of himself in this—whatever this was that they shared—seemed right.

It didn't mean he had to tell her his deepest, darkest secrets. They were still his own. He could invest in their connection, their friendship, without bringing his mistakes into the mix. There were other parts of himself he could share.

Parts he knew she liked.

"Oh, I want to stay." He drew her close to drag his mouth down her throat. Hell yeah. He wanted to stay for purely positive reasons. And not just for himself.

He wanted to show her it was okay to let her guard down a little. Loosen up. Enjoy each other's company. All without interruption.

She smiled. "I'm glad."

Leo studied Kaydee's face under the ambient light in the hall. She needed a better light. He mentally added it to his list. But tonight wasn't about repairs—at least, not home repairs. And he refused to think beyond that, or he'd have to deal with emotional bullshit. "So am I."

He shoved his hands in her hair and kissed her, slow at first, wanting to savor her warm sighs and the way she melted against him. But when she pressed her tongue to his, he shifted gears, tasting and taking and needing…everything.

When he finally broke for air, he helped her remove his shirt, which she'd already unbuttoned. Then he grabbed two handfuls of her dress, and damn…his whole body tightened at the low, needy sounds she made as he dragged the dress slowly over her peaked nipples.

"God…you're gorgeous," he murmured, dipping down to kiss each puckered tip while he continued to tug her dress completely off.

She hissed a breath and arched forward, shoving more of her delectable curves into his mouth. She already had him hard and throbbing. He needed more. Much more. Releasing her, he twisted her around and nuzzled the back of her neck.

"Leo," she whispered in a low, needy tone, lifting her arms to reach back and shove her hands in his hair.

Never one to waste an opportunity, he brought his hands around to fill his palms with her softness and groaned when she pressed her gorgeous ass against his erection.

Christ, she was killing him.

Kaydee was exquisite and matched his needs in so many ways. He wanted to make the night special for her. He wanted to reward her for her willingness to share her bed. Her night. And her morning with him.

He was going to satisfy them over and over, all night long, until they fell into an exhausted sleep. And woke up to do it all again. And again.

So he did.

. . .

Early the next morning, Kaydee woke up, warm and toasty, and deliciously sore in all the right places. Leo was good at that. So decadently good. He was also flat on his back, and she was sprawled all over him with her face smooshed into the crook of his neck.

Slowly lifting up, she watched him for signs of consciousness and couldn't stop the satisfaction warming her veins. He was out cold. This sexy, badass former Army Ranger was down for the count because of her. She might've broken him. Last night had been...wow.

And even though it'd been their first time spending the whole night together, technically, there'd been very little actual sleep involved. It seemed as if by taking that step, she'd dropped more than a little of her guard. Her inhibitions had hit the dust, too, because damn...last night had been round after mind-blowing round of hot, erotic, sensual sex unlike anything she'd ever experienced.

It didn't take much imagination to envision more mornings like this with him in her bed. Her stomach fluttered, but her chest tightened. Was this smart? Were they now on an unavoidable path to getting hurt?

Besieged with a swift onslaught of uncertainty, she

carefully eased out of bed and dashed into her bathroom. Had she made a mistake? Maybe she should've sent him to a hotel. She glanced in the mirror, as if it were magical and held the answers…and she blinked at her reflection. Her face was flushed, and her eyes were dazed, and she was…smiling?

Damn, she was. She really was…and couldn't wipe it off her face. That's because she felt amazing. And exceedingly happy. And she needed to embrace the opportunity she'd set in motion. The world didn't end because she let him stay, and he never pressured her about committing to anything. It made her realize there was no reason they couldn't continue their casual thing while including more delicious sleepovers.

So there would be no more running from Leo. Not even any thoughts of running.

Except to her sexy human furnace currently asleep in her bed. She'd left the air on all night, and without Leo's warmth she was cold.

In a heartbeat, she opened the door, and in another, she crawled back in bed.

"Everything okay?" her furnace asked in a sexy, sleepy tone that immediately woke her good parts, and she sighed when he pulled her in close.

"Mmm…there's a man in my bed," she said, snuggling closer, running her hand over the ridges of his abs…and farther south. "A hot, hard man."

"Your fault," he said, then muttered an oath when she stroked him. He grew harder.

So she did it again, and rocked against him, loving the feel of his thick, hard thigh between hers. "You're right."

Growling, he flipped them, tucking her beneath him, before kissing a path down her throat, licking her collarbone, while his hand did some straying and stroking of its own.

She gasped and arched up into his touch. "You feel great."

"You're right." He repeated her words, setting his

forearms on either side of her head. "You do."

His wavy hair fell forward, as he stared down at her through eyes dark with heat. God...he was beautiful and simply took her breath. She traced her fingertip along his scruffy jaw and then lifted up to nip at his lower lip and suck it into her mouth.

A half groan, half growl rumbled in his throat. "Hold that thought."

He rolled off to quickly put on a condom before returning to settle his body between her legs. "Okay, continue that thought."

"Yes, sir." Instead of lifting up to meet his lips, she threaded her fingers through his hair and tugged until his mouth met her neck.

Without needing further instructions, he kissed and nipped his way to her ear. Damn, he made her hot. So hot.

"Love the feel of you," he said against her throat. At this, he aligned his erection to her center and thrust inside her.

She cried out with him, and their desire echoed around her room. So good. He felt so good. And so right. He slid one arm beneath her back and gripped her shoulder, while his other hand cupped her ass. It was as if he needed to get close. Connect tight.

Above her, Leo's eyes drifted shut, his expression raw, uninhibited pleasure. Exactly what she was feeling. The way he was making her feel. Then he began to move in slow, lazy thrusts, like he had all morning to love her.

Which he did. He had the whole blessed morning.

Morning sex with Leo...

He was the reason she'd never done this before. The reason she'd never fallen asleep with a man. It was clear to her now. So clear.

She'd waited for him.

And damn, he was so worth the wait.

· · ·

Breakfast was over, and two of his buddies and their women were out front in the driveway when Leo arrived at the ranch on Monday. Normally, he would've been home last night, but in a sense, that was exactly where he'd been...buried deep inside Kaydee's soft curves, surrounded by her warmth and unyielding acceptance. Both physically and figuratively.

Home.

And damn, he just hadn't wanted to leave. So he hadn't.

Until this morning.

"Look what the cow dragged home," Vince said as Leo got out of his truck.

"Cow?" Jovy stiffened next to Stone and glanced around. "Is she here? I didn't hear her bell."

Leo snickered. Lula Belle was in love with Jovy's husband and didn't want to share him. The cow was always getting loose from her owner down the road and showing up at the ranch to see Stone and to make trouble for his wife. It was funny as hell. Although not for Jovy.

"Relax, hun." Stone slung his arm around her. "She's not here. Vince was speaking metaphorically."

"Yeah. That," Vince said, also standing with his arm around his woman. "I meant it was interesting to see Leo coming home in the morning, and with another smile on his face."

Shit. He might've known he wasn't going to get out of this without Chuckles saying something.

"You're right, he is smiling again," Stone said.

Vince grinned. "I think I even heard him whistling when he got out."

Leo snorted as he leaned against his truck. "You're full of shit. I wasn't whistling." At least, he didn't think so.

"But you *are* smiling," Stone said again, waving a hand

at him.

"*Still* smiling," Vince pointed out.

"Don't listen to them, Leo," Jovy said. "I think it's great Kaydee gives you a reason to smile. She does, doesn't she?"

He wasn't surprised she'd known about Kaydee. Apparently it hadn't taken his buddies long to tell their women about her.

He nodded. "Several reasons." And last night, she'd given him several new ones. The amazing woman was full of surprises…and limber. Christ she was so damn limber.

His mind immediately recalled an image of her, one that made him actually grateful for his photographic memory. The sight of her with one leg around his hip and the other stretched up the length of his torso as he leaned all the way over her was something he never wanted to forget. Nor was her gorgeous breasts bouncing in an erotic north-south motion while he drove into her until they were completely spent and boneless.

"Aww, that's wonderful," Emma gushed, moving closer.

Damn straight, but the hard-on he was sporting right now…not so much. He shifted to relieve some of the pressure.

"I'm glad for you," she continued, reaching out to squeeze his arm. "When do we get to meet her?"

Vince's grin broadened. "You should invite her over for brunch this Sunday."

"We'd love to meet her," Jovy said.

"Yeah," Stone said.

Emma patted his arm. "I think she'd be happy if you shared all this with her. But it's okay if you aren't ready."

Not ready for what? To share the ranch with Kaydee?

A year ago, he would've immediately vetoed the thought. Two years ago, it never would've even been a thought. But today—right now—he found himself actually embracing the thought. He was proud of At-Ease and the work he did here.

The veterans. His friends. All of it. And just because he and Kaydee weren't long term didn't mean he couldn't share this part of his life with her.

"Okay," he said. "I'll ask her."

"That's great." Emma squeezed his arm again.

"But don't get ahead of yourselves," he said. "There's a chance she won't want to come." His chest tightened at the thought, and it made him realize how much the woman meant to him. That only increased the tightness in chest.

"She'll come." Emma patted his arm again before releasing him.

Jovy smiled at him. "Emma's right. She'll come. And I think it's great."

A little uncomfortable now with their scrutiny, he shifted his weight and turned to Vince. "How's your house coming along?"

"It's halfway done." Vince's expression brightened further...if that was possible. "We're almost to the kitchen phase."

Happy for his buddy and Emma, and to have switched the focus off himself, he grinned. "That's good news." They deserved this.

"Speaking of kitchens," Stone said, gaining Leo's attention, "you remember Blanche from V-Spot, right?"

V-Spot was a restaurant Jovy once owned. Blanche used to work for her but was now part owner. "Yeah, I remember her."

"Well, she asked me to give her a kitchen estimate last week," Stone said. "She hired us last night. I'd like you to do the job."

Him? A job for someone he knew? A friend of the boss's wife? This was different. More at stake. More pressure. And damn if he wasn't honored that Stone was trusting him with this job. "Thanks," he said, straightening from the truck, a smile tugging his lips hard. "When does she want us to start?" By *us*, he meant him and his crew. The one milling around near the tool barn with the other crews.

Stone grinned. "Today. Come on inside. I'll show you the plans."

And then later, Leo was damn sure going to share those plans with his crew. No way would he make that mistake again. He was determined to make sure this job went smoother.

Especially since it was a job for a friend.

Chapter Thirteen

Tuesday evening, Kaydee pulled into the rec center parking lot with Fiona. Their first haircut clinic started in less than an hour and they wanted to get things set up. Hopefully, they'd gotten enough word out. Tonight's donations would go to the rec center to support senior activities. It would suck if no one showed.

She opened the back of her SUV so they could grab their equipment. Unsure what was needed, they packed their rolling cases with all the essentials before leaving the shop that afternoon. On the flyers, they'd only advertised free haircuts. After tonight, she figured they'd have a better idea what services were needed.

"How many people do you think will show?" Fi asked as they rolled their cases inside and down the hall to their assigned room, greeting a few people along the way. They'd requested the corner one because it was off by itself and had a tile floor for easier sweep-up.

She shrugged. "I don't really know. I'll be happy if at least two people show."

"Me, too," Fi said. "But I think we'll get more."

They spent the next half hour rearranging the room and setting out their equipment. Excitement skittered down her spine. It was actually happening. The clinic they'd lobbied for was starting in less than fifteen minutes.

"I think we're just about ready," Fiona said, glancing around the room. "I'm so glad Leo pushed you to act on your idea."

She grinned. "Me, too."

She was glad about a lot of things where that man was concerned. He made her feel things, both physically and emotionally, and although some of it scared the living daylights out of her, all of it made her feel alive. And that was addicting.

Fiona cocked her head and a smile tugged at her lips. "He agrees with you."

Kaydee straightened and glanced around. "He's here?" Her heartbeat increased, because, yeah, he affected that, too. "Where?"

"No." Fi laughed. "Leo's not here. I meant he's good for you. You're happier. Always smiling. In fact, I don't think you've stopped smiling the last two days."

She snorted. "I did so." Probably. Maybe. "I think."

Her friend laughed. "It's a good thing. I'm glad you're giving him a chance."

Opening up was scary, but the more she did, the more he did, and the more she wanted. Kaydee was in a strange, wonderful place in her life, and scared to death, yet excited.

"Regular orgasms from a guy you like to spend time with out of bed is rare." Fiona winked at her. "You hold on to him."

Kaydee blinked and was about to remind her friend where they were when several seniors entered the room.

"Are we in the right place for the free haircuts?" one of the gentleman asked.

"Yes, you are," she said, and spent the next hour and a half cutting hair.

After finishing her conversation with a nice little old lady—who not only needed a haircut, but someone to talk to about her dog and two cats—Kaydee swept up her area. She and Fiona had been going nonstop, but there was a lull in the action now, which afforded her a few minutes to sit and enjoy a cup of coffee.

"Don't get too comfortable," Fiona said with a grin. "Looks like you've got a special customer."

Special? How?

Curious about her friend's words and mischievous tone, she glanced around the woman to look at the doorway and sucked in a breath. "Leo." Joy ricocheted through her at the sight of the handsome blue-eyed man and propelled her to her feet.

Meeting her halfway, he pulled her in for a quick kiss to which both Fiona and the lady in her friend's chair echoed each other with an "aww."

Still in his arms, she smiled at him. "What are you doing here?"

"I came to support your first night," he said, his warm gaze doing funny things to her chest. "Do you have time to cut my hair?"

Her eyes widened. "Y-you want me to cut your hair?"

"Yes."

Now she blinked. It wasn't lost on her that the fact that he was willing to cut his hair was actually a big deal. A really big deal. His grandmother had told her he hadn't cut it since he left the military.

This told Kaydee a lot. She'd always gotten the impression it outwardly showed the world he hadn't cared about anything. She knew people hung on to hairstyles as a way to hold on to their past. So if Leo was willing to cut his hair, maybe he was ready to move forward.

To cut his link to the past.

"It's time." He continued to grin. "So...will you?"

"Of course she'll cut it," Fiona answered, and it knocked Kaydee out of her stupor.

She blinked. "Yes. Of course."

Her heart thudded hard as she took him by the hand and led him to her chair. Giving her this honor was huge. She wanted to do right by his trust. "What would you like me to do?"

He settled onto the metal chair and smiled his sexy damn smile, the one that made her weak in the knees. "You can do whatever you like to me."

Well hell.

Now she couldn't feel her legs. And Fiona and her client didn't help. Not with their soft sighs and "oh mys."

When she finally remembered how to breathe, Kaydee did some smiling of her own and held his gaze. "Good to know."

Although she had a lot of experience running her fingers through his silky hair and gripping tight while he kissed her long and deep and not so sweet, this time she kept her ministration on the professional side and assessed him with a critical eye.

Yep. He was gorgeous.

Leo had the right hair texture and amount of forehead to wear a short or long style. Since she loved his sexy, badass look, she decided to only trim a few inches off the bottom and shape the rest, being sure to leave enough for her to grip in the future.

Wetting his hair with her spray bottle, she tried not to think about the trust he'd just given her, but she failed. He was ready to shed his past, to shake off the very thing born from his self-induced purgatory, and he wanted *her* help.

The momentousness of it all hit Kaydee like a ton of bricks, and she had to blink away a sudden onslaught of tears.

Big, firm hands curled around her hips and squeezed. "You okay?"

Shoot. He was too astute. He noticed. And his concern only increased the burning behind her eyelids. She blinked again and nodded. Talking was out of the question at the moment, due to her hot throat, swollen with emotions best left unvoiced. Especially since they weren't alone. He was making her feel things and want things that were starting to seem like a good idea.

"Is now a bad time to ask you to come to At-Ease for brunch this Sunday?"

Her eyes went wide again, and she stopped cutting. "You want me to come to your ranch?"

"Yeah." He smiled, that sexy damn smile. "I'd like you to meet my friends and to show you around."

Her heart tried to jump into her swollen throat but kind of bounced instead. He wanted to share the things that meant the most to him…with her. The amazing man was wearing her down, knocking away all her barriers. Making it near impossible for her not to fall for him. "Yes. I'd like that."

She hoped to God she wasn't making a mistake.

• • •

Ever since the night of the haircut clinic, when Leo not only asked her to cut his hair, he asked her to visit his ranch, butterflies resided in Kaydee's stomach. And now it was Sunday, and he was driving them through Joyful, a town with quaint little shops lining each side of the main street, and those darn butterflies were going batshit crazy.

She'd been to Joyful before with Fiona. They'd heard about a gluten-free and vegan café in the paper and wanted to give it a try. The V-Spot was every bit as good as boasted. They'd enjoyed their lunch and had tentative plans to come down again next month.

But as Leo drove past the café, her mind wasn't on food. It was on the ranch and his army buddies, and the fact that he wanted to share them with her. Share his world. He was shedding his past and…God, she couldn't be more proud of him. Warmth funneled through her chest. She felt privileged, honored if she had any kind of part in it. That was a good thing. A *great* thing. So was the overnight bag he asked her to bring.

She brushed imaginary lint off the skirt of her sundress and concentrated on the color. It was a gorgeous shade of blue that reminded her of Leo's eyes. It calmed her.

Still, this was a huge step. One that excited and terrified her. She'd never gotten this far in a relationship. She usually bailed before this point. But she didn't want to bail this time.

The thought of it made her stomach ache almost as much as her chest. So, no. She wasn't going anywhere. She wasn't leaving. Not Leo. She loved being with him. He made her smile. Made her heart race. Made her body quiver with so much pleasure she sometimes forgot how to breathe.

That wasn't something she wanted to stop. Ever.

He reached over and covered her hand to halt her movements. She hadn't realized she was still brushing her skirt. His touch was warm and firm, and his strength seeped into her body like a much-needed spring thawing.

"You're thinking too loud," he said. "There's no need to stress. It's going to be fine. *You're* going to do fine."

She blew out a breath. "I just want your friends to like me."

Dammit. It felt like she was a teenager in a new school all over again.

He turned onto a country road and slowed down.

"Kaydee." His hold tightened on her hand and continued to do so until she met his gaze. "They're not going to like you. They're going to love you like..." He paused and blinked as a dazed look came into his eyes. Then he blinked again, and they cleared. "Like crazy."

She smiled. "Okay. Good. I'm so happy you asked me to come. I just don't want to screw it up."

"You could never do that." He brought one of her hands to his lips and kissed it.

She opened her mouth to respond, but movement outside caught her eye. "Um...there's a guy walking a...cow?"

Chapter Fourteen

A very *good*-looking guy, and a very big cow.

Leo turned to look, then laughed. "That's Stone and Lula Belle. She has a thing for him and is always breaking through her fence down the road to look for him at the ranch."

Kaydee recognized the name. It was the one Leo mentioned the most out of his buddies. Well, that one and Vince. She returned his grin. "That's adorable."

He snickered. "Tell that to Jovy, his wife. Lula Belle is not a fan."

Now *that* was funny.

"I better give him a hand," he said, pulling off to the side.

They got out and crossed the quiet road to join his buddy on the other side, and as Kaydee neared, she understood the cow's fascination with the guy. Stone was even better-looking up close. No wonder the cutie followed him around. She'd swoon, too, if her heart hadn't already belonged to Leo.

As that thought sank in, her heart dropped into her fluttering stomach. The heart that belonged to Leo. The sometimes brooding, sometimes charming, and always sexy former Army Ranger had broken through her walls and captured her heart. Once again, she was both happy and terrified, and…wow…she had absolutely no idea what to do with that information.

For now, she'd concentrate on meeting his friend. And the cow.

"Hey, Stone," Leo said, then grabbed her hand and tugged her close. "This is Kaydee. Kaydee, my former squad leader, Stone."

"Nice to meet you, Kaydee." Stone grinned. "Nice to meet the reason Leo's been walking around with a smile on his face."

Fiona had been right about Leo smiling…and her being the cause. Warmth funneled through Kaydee's chest again and up into her cheeks.

"Good to meet you, too," she said. "And your cow."

Stone laughed. "Lula Belle is one headstrong female."

Leo snorted. "So's your wife." He nodded toward the cow. "What happened this time?"

Stone sighed and shook his head. "She trampled Jovy's petunias. Again."

"Again?" Kaydee asked and spent the next few minutes laughing until she cried as the two men regaled her with Jovy-versus-Lula Belle stories. "Man." She inhaled and wiped her wet face. "Sounds like there's never a dull moment."

Leo snickered. "There isn't."

And she could tell by the gleam in his eyes that it was a good thing.

"Looks like she got out down here," Stone said, walking toward a section of busted fence a few feet away.

Lula Belle followed, her tail swishing as she lumbered. And ten minutes later, the cow stood and mooed on the other side of the repaired fence, while they climbed into Leo's truck and headed for the ranch.

"Thanks for the help," Stone said as they drove down the road.

As hc and Leo chatted, Kaydee used the opportunity to take in the open fields surrounding the road, and the large oak trees dotting the landscape.

It was quiet and so darn peaceful. No wonder the town was named Joyful. It was fitting.

Leo's hand rested lightly on her knee, and the thin material of her sundress did little to stop his heat from seeping through to her skin, making her hyperaware of him.

Which normally was great, but not with his friend sitting on her other side. She inhaled slow and steady and pushed back her needs, and by the time they parked in front of a beautiful white two-story house with a large front porch, she was able to focus.

The main house, no doubt.

"This place is amazing," she said as Leo held out his hand and helped her from the truck.

To the left were several large buildings and two large barns. The ranch was bigger than she expected. At quick count, twenty-three people milled about. Some sat on benches near a large oak, others jogged—although she didn't know how in this heat, and yet they seemed unfazed. Three card games were going on at three different picnic tables. Two women sat reading up against the tree, and beyond that, she could see horses in a field, some with riders, others grazing.

All in all, the vibe was peaceful. At ease.

Exactly what the name promised.

"I'll give you a tour later," Leo said with a grin. "But right now, it's time to eat." Still holding her hand, he guided her toward the house behind Stone.

Once inside, she caught glimpses of wooden floors, Southwestern decor, and white walls. He ushered her past an office, a living room, and what appeared to be a large den or game room of sorts, with a vaulted, beamed ceiling. Then they took a left into a big dining room with two long tables with bench seating. Another quick head count came up with six. For some reason she expected the house to be teeming with people, too.

Leo must've read the surprise on her face because he explained, "The main breakfast for the ranch is over. Sunday brunch is the only time we eat separate from the rest."

"It gives us all a chance to catch up," Stone said, then his face lit up as a stunning dark-haired woman with beautiful blue eyes approached.

"There you are. I was beginning to think you got lost," the brunette said, and lifted up on tiptoe to kiss his cheek. "Lula Belle back safe and sound?"

"Yep." Stone smiled and pulled the woman in for a proper kiss that went on longer than Kaydee expected and had her glancing at Leo.

A smile tugged his lips. "They do that a lot."

When the two came up for air, Leo introduced her to Jovy, and soon she was surrounded by three other couples, all of whom appeared genuinely happy to meet her.

The incredibly handsome Italian gave her a bear hug and thanked her for putting life in Leo's eyes. His fiancée, Emma, echoed the sentiment. A large, handsome dark-haired Thor type introduced himself as "the better-looking Mitchum brother" before his beautiful green-eyed fiancée told her to ignore him and gave her a "welcome to the ranch" hug. She'd barely recovered when her heart stuttered for a split second as a Jensen Ackles look-alike shook her hand, and his pretty wife hugged her.

Then Leo's hand found hers, and he entwined their fingers. "I know they're a lot to take in."

She laughed, a little nervous, and a lot happy to be by his side. He got her. He understood the situation was a bit overwhelming. He was in tune with her inner makeup. Without thinking, she leaned in and kissed his cheek.

Whistles and catcalls echoed around them, and she felt her face heat, but laughed it off with the others as they all sat down. Except for Vince and Emma, who disappeared through a swinging door Kaydee assumed was the kitchen. A second later, they returned with their arms full of steaming dishes. She offered to help but was shot down by the smiling couple, and soon she was asking and answering questions while eating a plateful of delicious food.

When they were nearly done, Brick leaned around Leo to grin at her. "Are you responsible for turning him back into a man?"

Stone choked on a mouthful of food, and Emma spewed her iced tea all over poor Jovy, who unfortunately happened to be seated across from her. Jovy just laughed as she wiped the tea off her face and neck, and good-naturedly insisted Emma not worry about it.

Grateful she had nothing in her mouth at the time, Kaydee picked up on the teasing tone and smiled at Brick. "Trust me. Leo's all man. Always has been."

Leo's hand settled on her leg and squeezed while he and the others chuckled.

"Actually, Kaydee," Beth said, craning her head around Brick to look at her. "I was dying to ask you about Leo's hair, too, just in a nicer way than my handsome goof. Are you responsible for the gorgeous cut?"

The compliment brought a flush of heat to her face. "Yes," she answered. "Leo stopped by the rec center to support me during our first haircut clinic."

"Haircut clinic?" Brick frowned at her. "Is that where you teach him to cut hair?"

She chuckled. "No." Then explained the concept to everyone, including how Leo was responsible for encouraging her to submit the proposal in the first place.

"So you and your friend cut hair for free, and the customers leave a donation and all the proceeds go to support a cause?" Stone asked.

"Yes." She nodded.

"I freakin' love that." Jovy's gaze was bright as she smiled at her. "Would you consider doing that here? Not for charity. Just free haircuts for the vets. But we'd pay you, of course."

"Oh, I couldn't take any money," she said with a shake of her head. Fiona wouldn't want to, either. "But I'd be happy to donate my time, and I'm sure my friend would, too. So… sure."

Stone shook his head. "No. We'll pay you."

"But I wouldn't feel right," she insisted.

"Neither would I," Jovy said. "Use the money as an investment toward your friend's shop."

Fi's shop?

Raising a brow, she glanced at Leo. He told them? He actually talked to them about her and Fiona?

"Yes." He smiled. "They know about your search for commercial space. I'm proud of you for helping your friend, and for going after what you want at the rec center."

And she knew this to be true, because she saw it reflected in his eyes. "Thanks." Warmed by his pleased look, she covered his hand with hers and didn't think her chest could expand any further.

Jovy continued to smile at her. "So…will you help us out and let us help you out?"

The woman sure was persistent. And kind. And Kaydee caved. She agreed to contact Jovy later that week, after she talked to Fiona.

The rest of brunch went by fast, with the women filling her in on how they met their guys, and before she knew it, someone shoved a giant mouthwatering piece of chocolate cake in front of her.

Kaydee moaned. "What is this place? Shangri-la?"

"Close." Beth chuckled. "Wait until you taste it. Emma's cakes rock."

Kaydee would've agreed, but once she took a bite, she didn't come up for air until it was gone.

"I've been thinking," Leo began.

Brick snorted. "Bet that hurt."

Holding a hand up to Brick, Leo cupped it with his other, no doubt to shield the fact that he was flipping the guy off. When Brick's chuckle confirmed it, Kaydee smiled. Everyone was so at ease with one another here. She relaxed in her chair and enjoyed the exchange.

Leo turned his attention back to Stone. "Ever think about building a proper mess hall here?" The room grew silent. Even his goofy friend sobered. "Maybe use my money to build it. This way Vince and Emma would have an industrial kitchen to cook and bake in."

"Damn...that would be great," Vince said with a grin.

Leo sat back. "And I'm betting more veterans would show up to eat."

"They would?" Stone frowned from across the table. "Why do you think that?"

He cleared his throat. "I know from experience that it's a little too intimate in here. I mean, we're inside a house. *Your* house, Stone. Granted, your dining room here is big, and the long tables and benches help, but it can still be off-putting when you're in military mode...or living with demons in your head. It's not a place you want to be when you're not up to socializing."

Kaydee's chest squeezed.

At the rec center months ago, she'd overheard about Leo's past, and yet his tone and his words about broke her heart. God, she hated the thought of him ever feeling the way he just described. She knew this had happened before they'd met, but still, she thought back over the past several months, recalling their encounters. He never gave any signs of feeling that way. God…if he had, she would've done something. What? She had no idea, but she never would've sat by and let him go through that alone.

Inhaling slowly, she clenched her jaw and fought the onslaught of tears, knowing he absolutely would not want them. But she squeezed his hand, needing to convey to him that she was there for him. He squeezed back.

"Huh." Stone ran a hand through his hair. "I never thought about it like that."

The more Leo talked, the more she fell for the man. "We can make the mess hall wheelchair accessible. With a lot more tables, so if anyone wants to sit alone, they can, or if they want to join others, they can do that, too."

"They'll have a choice," Brick said.

Leo turned to his buddy and nodded. "Exactly."

"This is a real good idea, Leo," Cord said.

"Damn good." Stone smiled and turned his attention to Vince. "I'll need you to sit down with me and tell me what you'll need, then I'll crunch numbers with Jovy and draw it up."

As they talked shop a little more, her mind fuzzed over with thoughts of how much she admired Leo.

Big-time.

The rest of the day and all through the evening, those thoughts stayed uppermost in her mind. During her tour, their horseback ride and picnic, supper, and even now as they hung out in the game room with the other couples and played a round of darts. Something she was actually good at.

"You should've warned us you had a ringer," Brick said to Leo, after she placed all three of her darts in the three-point area and won the game.

Stone snorted. "She wouldn't be a ringer if he told you,

dumbass. Ringers are secrets."

"True." Leo chuckled, sliding his arm around her waist and dragging her in close. "But you're giving me too much credit. I didn't know Kaydee was this good."

"He's right," she said. "We've never played before."

At least…not darts. She held back a grin, but Leo didn't. He smiled outright, and heaven help her, his gaze smoldered behind his amusement. The sudden urge to strip him naked and lick him from toe to head rippled through her.

He must've read the intent in her eyes, because his smile disappeared, and he straightened. "Well…time to turn in. It's late."

Brick glanced at the clock over the bar and frowned. "It's not even eight."

"It is in Philly," Jovy said.

Leo nodded. "Good enough."

Laughter echoed through the room as his hand pressed into the small of her back and he guided her toward the door.

"Good night," she managed to say.

They entered the hall and headed toward the stairs. She should probably be embarrassed. It had to be obvious to his friends where they were going and what they were about to do. But since she knew the endgame, she was more excited than mortified. The instant they were out of view of the room, he crushed her close and kissed the strength from her legs.

Leo's specialty.

He released her mouth and kissed his way to her ear. "God, I want you." His words and the need in his tone made her tremble.

She clung to him to keep from falling. "I want you, too," she said, her voice breathless and low. "Where's your room?"

"Upstairs." He swept her into his arms and took the steps at a fast pace, not slowing until he strode down a hall and entered a room.

"Hey." She laughed. "Save some of that energy."

Chuckling, he shut the door with his foot. "Think you know that's never been a problem, but I'm more than happy to remind you. All night."

"All night?" Heat flooded her belly. Another all-nighter with Leo sounded like heaven. She wasn't going to want to leave his bed. "But my bag—"

"Is already up here, so we have no reason to leave."

Leaning close, she breathed him in. The smell of soap still lingered on his skin. Inhaling again, she kissed a path along his jaw, nipping at his chin on the way to his mouth. "Good," she said, brushing his lips.

He let her body slide down his until her feet hit the floor. She moaned.

Damn, he was hard. Everywhere.

His body was solid and muscular and felt amazing against hers. She rocked into him, and he muttered an oath. So she did it again. And still again. He growled before pressing her against the wall and trapping her with that incredible body as he took possession of her mouth.

His kiss was hungry and demanding, and heat rushed through her so hot and fast she shook with raw need. Never in her life had she ever burned for someone. But she burned for Leo. Burned bad.

"I swear I'm going to combust," she uttered when he broke the kiss. "I need you in me now."

He smiled a sexy, badass smile and gathered the skirt of her dress in his hands and lifted it up and over her head. And then her strapless bra was gone, too. "Love these," he said, hooking his thumbs in her pale blue bikini-cut panties and tugging them off. Glancing down at what he'd revealed, Leo growled. "Finally," he said roughly, lifting her up to carry her to his bed and set her gently on the mattress. "Been waiting all damn day to get you naked."

Chapter Fifteen

For a moment, she thought he was going to skip the preface and sink right into her body. But he climbed on the bed with her and kissed his way down her throat to a breast, dragging a hoarse moan from her as she arched up into him.

With a groan, he nuzzled and kissed his way to her other breast, his muscular, decadent body giving off so much heat she felt it through his clothes. Needing to feel skin, nothing but his skin, she tugged at his shirt. "Off. Everything off."

He stood, and with his eyes on her, he began to strip, kicking off his shoes and yanking the shirt over his head. The sight of his rippling muscles made her mouth water. He fished a condom from his pocket and tossed it on the bed. Another hit the mattress a second later.

She arched a brow. "Feeling frisky, are you?"

"Damn straight," he muttered, removing his jeans and socks.

"Finally." She ran her gaze down, then back up, his magnificent body. "Been waiting all damn day to get you naked," she said, repeating his words with a grin.

Chuckling, he bent down to kiss her ankle and used his shoulders to spread her legs as his mouth took the scenic route north. By the time he arrived at her inner thigh she was trembling. He kissed first one. And then the other. And then…in between.

Kaydee gripped the comforter in her hands as she rocked up into him, and when his tongue flicked over her, she cried out, hoping no one was upstairs because she wasn't exactly quiet.

Unconcerned, he slid his deliciously calloused hands beneath her. "Watch," he said, and brought her to his mouth.

Biting her lips, she watched his broad shoulders wedge her thighs wider. Watched the sleek muscles in his back ripple and flex with his movements. Watched pleasure deepen the blue of his eyes before they drifted shut, and he moaned at the taste of her.

And when he sucked her sensitized nub into his mouth, it all became too much. Watching was no longer possible because her eyes rolled back in her head as she came. Hard. And then, because he didn't let her go, the talented man somehow made her come again.

• • •

Only when she was completely boneless did Leo swipe a condom from the mattress and roll it on. Her breathing was still erratic, and it thrilled the hell out of him that he could wreck her like she wrecked him.

"You're so beautiful," he told her, kissing his way up her body. She made him want things. Made him feel things. Normally, that would produce a red flag, and he'd run for the hills.

But not with Kaydee. Never with Kaydee.

He brushed her mouth with his, first one corner, then

the other, before trailing down to her neck, shocked at the emotions she brought to his surface.

Earlier that day, when they were driving through Joyful, he realized just how strong those emotions were and almost told her. But he wasn't ready to say it out loud. He needed to live with it a little. Hell, just admitting to himself that his feelings for Kaydee were strong was a big-ass step.

"Leo—"

"I know," he said, feeling incredibly naked. Raw. One hundred percent open. But he relaxed, and by doing that right here, right now, with Kaydee, allowing whatever was meant to happen…happen, it felt…freeing.

So damn freeing.

His worries began to slide away. His secret fears. Even his demons went silent. "Just let go, Kaydee. Give me everything. Give me you."

And then lifting up, he held her gaze as he nudged her legs farther apart with his hips and thrust inside her. All the air left his body, and she was saying his name over and over again. And in spite of himself, his secrets, and his fear of what was going to happen when she found out the truth about him, in spite of it all, he was most definitely falling in love with her.

"Leo," she whispered in a low, sultry tone that had heat gripping his spine.

She pulled him closer, digging her nails into his back as he rocked her through another orgasm. Pulsing, throbbing, she felt so fucking good tightening around him again and again. He dipped down to capture her cries in a kiss he needed to take and taste as he raced to his own release. She met every one of his thrusts with an equally fierce out-of-control passion, and it sent him over the edge.

Afterward, they lay there, breathing heavy, his body still deep inside hers, and he didn't move other than to brace himself up enough to let her breathe. He didn't want to pull out yet. She felt like heaven. Pure heaven. Her hands were still around his back, clutching his shoulder blades, and he could feel her heart pounding against his chest. He was grateful they didn't need to move, because he didn't want to let her go.

But when a few more minutes went by and she still didn't stir or say anything, he rolled to the side and brushed his mouth across her damp temple. "You okay?" His voice was hoarse but audible.

She nodded, and her contented sigh filled the air between them. "I can't believe it's always going to be like that."

"Like what?"

He knew what it was like for him. Incredible. Spine-melting. World-rocking. But he suddenly needed to know how she felt.

"Like it's the very best thing ever. Lottery-winning best thing." Satisfaction softened her tone, and she yawned. "And I don't want it to end."

Very on board with that analogy and sentiment, he kissed her temple again. Considering she was the "didn't do permanent" type, that admittance told him she was definitely feeling things as deeply as he. Smiling, he made a quick trip to the bathroom to take care of business, then returned to bed, gathered her close, and yanked the comforter over them. It was great to know he wasn't in this craziness alone. She snuggled into him and sighed.

He had never brought a woman to the ranch before. Never had a woman in this bed before. Never wanted a woman here.

Until Kaydee.

She was special. Special enough to get him to cut his hair without even asking. It'd been his decision. He had no need for the armor anymore. He wasn't the man he used to be. It'd been time to cut loose from the past. What better time to do it than to support Kaydee, the woman who saw him as a solid man? The kind he should've been. The kind he used to be before shit hit the fan overseas. The kind he wanted to be again.

A man she could admire.

A man deserving of her.

He was working on it. A modicum of confidence and self-respect expanded his chest. He was making progress, too. Was it enough?

He hoped so. Once he confessed his feelings to her, and if they were reciprocated, there was no way he could keep his past from her.

His last thought before exhaustion claimed him was that he didn't want her to leave and hoped he was enough to satisfy her restlessness.

• • •

After work on Tuesday, Kaydee and Fiona went to check out yet another storefront. She'd lost count of how many that made. Too many. All of them a waste of time. Including, unfortunately, tonight's fiasco.

"Rats?" Fiona shivered. "Can you believe he showed us a place with rats? Hell to the no!"

"I was done before we entered," Kaydee said as she drove them back through town toward Yellow Rose, where Fiona had left her car. "The bars on the windows—"

"Windows?" Fi cut her off. "There wasn't any glass. Not unless you count plywood as glass."

She snickered. "Nope."

"Me, either." Her friend sighed. "I'm beginning to think there aren't any places out there for us."

"Us?" Kaydee frowned.

"Yes, *us*." Fi held up a hand. "I know you don't want to be a partner and make a commitment to staying, but I thought perhaps you'd at least consider working *for* me. You can just as easily pick up and leave my shop when your dad retires as you can Rose's."

True. She blinked. Once Fi actually opened her shop and left Yellow Rose, Kaydee would miss her friend. Unless Kaydee left, too.

"Does your silence mean you're considering it?" Fiona smiled expectantly at her.

She slowly grinned. "Yeah. I'll consider it." Working for Fi was actually a pretty good idea.

"Super!" Fiona clasped her hands together. "Now, if I could just get fate to climb on board, that'd be great, too."

Kaydee silently agreed. It was as if fate conspired against Fi. Didn't want her friend to strike out on her own. How the hell hard could it be to find something the woman could afford that wasn't a danger to anyone's well-being?

Apparently, really hard.

"Maybe I should consider going to Joyful," Fiona said. "I mean, I do like the town. It's cute. And your boyfriend's buddies own commercial property."

Her boyfriend...

Just hearing that term in relation to Leo sent those darn butterflies in motion again. They made her a little queasy.

"Joyful is only an hour from here," Fi continued. "I mean, it's not horrible. It's mostly highway driving."

"It would mean a longer commute for you, though."

Fiona shrugged. "Maybe for me, but I'm sure you could stay with Mr. Winter Soldier."

She laughed. "Don't let him hear you call him that. I think he's heard it too much."

"Sucks to be him." Grinning, Fiona waved her hand. "Looking like a handsome movie star. Yeah. That's a tough cross to bear."

Kaydee sobered. The guy had weathered some damn heavy crosses in his life. He didn't need any more. "I wouldn't move there. I have to stay with my grandfather until my dad retires."

She slowed down as she neared the salon parking lot. It was deserted except for two cars, and the lights were on in the shop, which she and Fiona closed and locked up an hour ago.

Fiona frowned. "Why is Rose here?"

Kaydee shut the engine off. "Don't know. Let's go find out."

"There you two are," Rose said, standing next to her husband behind the counter, both wearing matching grins.

"Okay...what's going on?" Fiona frowned, glancing back and forth. "Are we on *Candid Camera*? Or something?"

"No, honey." Rose shook her head as she came around the counter, smile still curving her lips. "Earl and I have a proposition for you."

"Me?" Fiona raised her brows.

"Yes." The older man moved to slide an arm around his wife. "We know you want to own your own shop, and I've finally convinced Rose to hang up her scissors and see the country with me."

Rose snickered. "While we're still young enough to get around on our own."

"So...what exactly are you saying?" Kaydee asked, not daring to believe what her gut was telling her.

"We want to sell the salon to Fiona."

"*Punk'd*," Fi said, glancing around again. "We're on *Punk'd*, right?"

Earl laughed. "No."

Her friend stilled, and Fiona's eyes widened. "S-o-o... you're for real?"

"Yes." Rose chuckled.

Fiona let out a high-pitched *whoop* and pulled Rose in for a hug. "I'll take it."

Their boss laughed. "Don't you want to hear our

proposition first?"

"Of course," Fi said.

"Great." Earl motioned with his hand toward the back of the shop. "Let's go to the office and talk numbers. Trust me. It's doable."

Excitement propelled Kaydee forward. She did trust them, and for the first time since she started to help Fi salon-shop, she had a good feeling about this one. Neither of them was going to have to leave this location. Warmth radiated throughout her body. For someone who embraced and encouraged changes, she was surprisingly happy her work and personal relationships were heading in a more permanent direction.

Life was good. God, it'd be great if it stayed that way.

Chapter Sixteen

Ever since that first morning Leo woke up in his bed at the ranch with Kaydee in his arms, he'd felt different. Centered.

Grounded.

Over the past week and a half, they'd fallen into a very satisfying, comfortable routine. And she seemed different, too. More relaxed. Open. And that was before her friend had signed papers to buy Yellow Rose Salon. Although that definitely put a smile on her face. He loved seeing her so happy. He'd given her another reason to smile when they'd had their own private celebration over the weekend.

That was three days ago. He hadn't seen her since, and he admittedly missed her. Something he'd never felt with any other woman. Longing. It was kind of a double-edged sword. Sucked at the time, but when they did see each other their connection was stronger.

Thankfully, today was Wednesday, which meant his weekly trip north tonight to have dinner with his grandmother, followed by dessert with Kaydee. She was the dessert...and more. So much more. He still hadn't told her how he felt, though.

Admitting their feelings would be a step toward commitment. If that happened, he'd have to tell her about his past. He believed the only way a relationship could work was if it was open, and there were no secrets. Trouble was, revealing the secrets from his past could jeopardize his future with Kaydee. But not telling her would definitely doom his chance at a relationship with her.

The woman was worth the chance.

Still, it'd been tougher to get the words out than he'd thought…especially when she touched him. Once her hands were on his skin, he lost his ability to think straight.

But for now, he had work to concentrate on. So after his quick morning briefing with his crew—something he initiated after that disastrous first day—he headed for his truck. As soon as he opened the door, his phone rang.

Hoping it was Kaydee, he smiled and glanced at the phone, surprised to see "Mom" on the screen. They had their regular weekly Monday check-in two days ago.

"Hey, Mom," he greeted, climbing into the cab. "What's up? Something wrong?"

"That depends," she said.

His spine immediately stiffened. Not exactly a positive answer. "On what?" He shoved his keys in the ignition and clicked his seat belt in place but made no move to start the truck.

"If you'd mind checking on your grandmother for another few weeks," she said, her contrite tone filling his truck. "The twins are colicky, and your sister could use my help a little longer."

Smiling, he started the truck and headed to work. "That's fine. I don't mind."

His mother's sigh rustled through the phone. "Thanks, hun. I hate imposing on you. But at least your trips are…

okay. I hear you and Kaydee are getting cozy."

Unsure exactly what he was supposed to say to that, he decided to keep it truthful and short. "Yeah."

Didn't get any shorter than that. He bit back a laugh.

"I'm glad." Another sigh met his ear. "I like her."

He grinned. "So do I."

"That's good to hear. It makes me happy knowing you're happy. You deserve it, hun," she said, then let it drop, and the conversation switched to feedings, and spit-up, and damn, was Leo glad he could leave it behind when he hung up.

His mother was great, though. She was never the type to meddle. Although he knew she felt guilty for not prying when he'd first gotten back from active duty. He'd reassured her many times it wouldn't have mattered. Not one damn bit. Back then, he'd been a master at shutting everyone out.

Not now.

Thanks to therapy. His family. His friends.

And lately, thanks to Kaydee.

She managed to reach him more deeply than anyone. He planned to continue to see the amazing woman with or without grandma duty. That was, if she wanted to see him after tonight. Yeah. Tonight was the night. He was finally going to grow a damn pair and fucking tell her how he felt, and about his past.

It was time. He couldn't keep doing the things they were doing without being completely honest with her. Somehow, he'd find a way to suffer through her disappointment and hope she didn't kick him to the curb. The woman was always forthright and deserved the same treatment from him. He had to tell her.

But right now, he had to push those thoughts aside and once again switch back to work mode. Parking in Blanche's driveway, he gave his head a mental shake and quickly brought today's checklist to mind. *Install the countertops when they're delivered this morning.*

He'd lucked out on this assignment. Blanche and her husband were dream customers. Even his workers felt that way. Just yesterday, when he and his crew were installing the floors, they all agreed how great it would be to have more customers like the Parkers. He suspected it had to do with the tasty baked goods the woman left for them on the dining room table each morning before she headed to work. Within ten minutes the plate was always empty.

A smile tugged Leo's lips when he entered the house to find the guys chowing down on doughnuts.

Gluten-free ones.

He snickered. Even though the men knew Blanche was part owner of V-Spot, he doubted they realized the baked goods came from her café. They should, though. Poor woman's kitchen was currently nonexistent.

"Hey, boss, you might want to grab one of these while you can," Dirk said between bites. "Blanche outdid herself today."

"Okay." He swiped a doughnut off the plate and took a bite. *Cinnamon.* And as usual, damn good. There were only two left now. If Tucker didn't get his ass here soon he was shit out of luck. Everyone else was already here and devouring their treat.

The kid was usually the last one to arrive, preferring his bike to hitching a ride with him or the others. Leo suspected the young veteran still had trouble with confined spaces.

Hell, one tour would do it, and the kid had been on two.

Every so often, Tuck got a look on his face Leo recognized. Panic. He'd seen the wide, dark, and dazed gaze many times in his mirror in the past. Felt the constricted chest and labored breathing, and as if the skin was too tight for his face.

So when Tucker took one too many smoke breaks, Leo let him. He also got the kid to agree to sit in on this Friday's group therapy session with him. It meant a late arrival at his gram's, but she was already aware, and Kaydee told him not to worry about the seniors and bingo. She'd cover it.

And then he'd cover her.

At that delicious thought, his lips weren't the only thing to twitch.

"Damn, there's Tuck," Dirk grumbled at the sound of the bike pulling up outside. It meant he had to leave the last doughnut for the kid.

One of the other crew members cupped the big guy's shoulder. "Better luck next time."

Fifteen minutes later, Leo wished to God he'd had some of that luck when the countertop arrived. Blanche had wanted quartz.

The shop delivered granite.

What the hell?

Leo dialed the distributor as he strode outside, explaining the mix-up with a calm he was far from feeling.

"Hi, Mr. Reed," the woman who identified herself as Heather said in pleasant voice. "I remember you. Let me call up the order…okay…you originally ordered quartz, but then you called later that day to change it to granite."

What?

He stiffened and glanced around the front of Blanche's yard as if it held the answers. "No. I came into your shop with my order," he told her, gripping the phone as he worked to keep his irritation at bay.

"Yes, I know. I remember you," Heather said, her voice softening. "Then you called a few hours later and changed it to granite."

Like hell. Blanche wanted low maintenance. No sealing. Sanitary. No staining worries.

Quartz.

"I have it noted right here," she said, as if he could see

through the phone.

He jumped in his truck and cranked the engine. "I'll be right there."

Leo hung up without waiting for a reply. Dick move. He'd feel bad about it later. Right now, he needed answers. Doing his best to keep calm, he controlled his breathing and drove the twenty minutes to the manufacturer he'd visited ten days ago to place the damn quartz order.

They'd screwed up. Not him. He didn't call. Why the fuck would he?

Christ. This was just great. Fucking great. Another screwup. How the hell was he going to explain this cost and delay to Stone?

Maybe Blanche had changed the order…

A long shot, but he needed to find out.

Sucking it up, he called the woman and clenched his fist to keep his anger in check when she told him it wasn't her. She wanted quartz. He promised her he'd fix it. Then hung up.

He didn't fucking need this.

By the time he walked into the shop his gut was knotted tight, but he didn't show his aggravation. He was good at masking emotions, thanks to years of training and practice.

A half hour later, he left with the quartz countertop ordered, a new delivery date set for that Saturday, and a huge hit to his bank account to expedite things. No way would he allow Foxtrot to pay for his mistake.

And it was his mistake, because even though he didn't make that damn call and couldn't prove someone at the distributer screwed up, he was responsible for material orders.

On his way back to the jobsite, Leo stopped in at V-Spot to update Blanche. A stop he hadn't wanted to make. A fucking stop he shouldn't have *had* to make. As expected, though, she was nothing but nice, telling him it just meant she got out of cooking for a few more days.

But it wasn't right, and the more he thought about it, the more it aggravated him.

Pulling in front of Blanche's house, he slammed his truck in park as self-disgust mixed with stress to grip his shoulders and twist around his spine.

Twice now, he nearly ruined Foxtrot's name. Two screwups in only two jobs. Some goddamn supervisor he turned out to be. He was putting the company's and his buddies' reputations in jeopardy.

Once he finished Blanche's kitchen, Leo was going to think long and hard about telling Stone to find someone else to run the crew.

He was bad luck.

A burden.

Perhaps he was better off as a crew member, instead of a leader in a position to hurt Foxtrot.

Swallowing back a sour taste in his mouth, he forced himself to face a bitter truth. Maybe there were other things in his life he was fooling himself he could handle, too.

Chapter Seventeen

It still hadn't sunk in.

Two days ago, Kaydee watched Fiona sign papers to get the ball rolling on purchasing Yellow Rose from their boss. After talking with Rose and Earl last week, they all met again, but this time with business lawyers in attendance. Since the purchase price was well within Fi's preapproval amount for a business loan, and Rose had all her papers in order, it'd only taken her friend's lawyer a few days to go through everything and secure a good loan rate. So now Fi was just waiting on a call to let her know when she'd close.

In the meantime, it was work as usual. They both had a half shift today. Kaydee yawned. Normally, she liked to work eight-hour days, but those had been rare lately. Thankfully, today wasn't one of them. She only had an hour left. Which was good because…damn, she was still dog-tired from Sunday with Leo. Too much celebrating. She fought a grin. Nah, no such thing as too much Leo. He visited, but as usually happened when he stayed the night, there wasn't much sleep involved.

It was three days later, and she was still trying to play catch-up.

Kaydee yawned again—something she'd been doing a lot lately. Leo's fault. Her lips twitched, and warmth flooded her chest. Just thinking about him made her heart smile. And if that sentimental hoo-hah wasn't true, she'd probably puke.

But it was true. Every bit.

"Your young man is putting that smile on your face," Ida Nelson said as she sat waiting with her sister. The two women came in once a month to have their hair set and to gossip.

Kaydee was waiting for Fiona to finish the appointment she was on before the two of them tackled the sisters. They liked to sit under the dryers together, so there was no sense starting one until they could both be done.

"How do you know it's a man?" Olivia elbowed her sister. "Maybe it's a woman."

Kaydee's smile increased. "It's a guy." Leo was definitely all man.

"Ah, to be young and in love again," Ida said, a dreamy look coming into her eyes.

Or perhaps it was just cataracts.

It didn't matter. Kaydee's mind caught the L-word and stuck.

"Love?" Her heart dropped into her fluttering stomach.

What did she know about love? Other than for family and friends.

"Trust me, honey." Olivia had risen to her feet and stood in front of the counter smiling at her. "Any man who brings a flush to your cheeks and a soft look in your eyes is definitely someone you're in love with."

"In love?" With Leo. Kaydee blinked and sat back in her chair. Was she in love with him? She had no clue. She'd never been in love before. Never opened herself up for it.

"Does he make your heart flutter?" Ida asked, standing

next to her sister now.

"Do you miss him when he's not around?" Olivia asked.

Ida leaned closer. "Do you count the hours until you see him?"

All seemingly silly questions, but the thing was, Kaydee did do all three. "Yeah." She cleared her throat, feeling a little foolish having this conversation in public.

"Here's the kicker," Ida said, leaning closer still. "This one is the true test."

Olivia jerked her head toward her sister and snorted. "True test? What would you know of a true test? You haven't been in love for decades."

Kaydee smiled, enjoying the exchange between the women. It wasn't a far stretch to imagine her and Fiona carrying on like this when they were older. The fact that she'd have to stick around a long time to grow old with Fiona made her question why she even had the thought.

Leo's smiling face flashed through her mind. *He* was why she'd had a thought about the future here. His eyes held so much warmth her heart threatened to leave her chest.

Yeah, her new outlook was definitely his fault. Ever since they started dating, the incredible man had tipped her world on its axis, and now her view had changed. It had altered.

Like her.

This wasn't a bad thing, either. Just different. But still good. Great even.

Ida lifted her chin. "Only need to be in it once to know. The best way to tell if you're in love is this: If you close your eyes, can you picture your life without him?"

It was crazy. She didn't even need to close her eyes to answer that. It was as plain as the pain in her chest when she tried to breathe. "No," she said. "My answer's no. I don't even want to try to picture my life without him."

Once again, for someone who didn't do long term, this

was certainly a new path. An *altered* one.

Ida slapped the counter...pretty hard for a frail hand. "Then you're in love with him." The woman's gaze grew misty, and she placed her hand over Kaydee's. "Just don't make the mistake I did. Don't let him get away. Tell him how you feel. I should've told my Tommy, but I was young, and he was a white man. I listened to my parents when I should've listened to my heart."

By this time, Olivia had moved closer and put her arm around her sister. "I remember that. Is he the reason you never married?"

"Yes." Ida sighed. "He was my true love. And I let him slip through my fingers. No one could ever take his place."

Kaydee's heart squeezed for the poor woman, and the conversation stayed with her long after the sisters' hair had been set and they'd left. She didn't want to let Leo slip through her fingers.

God, no. She wanted to hold on to him with both hands. Tight. This new path she was on was just that...new. She had no idea how to keep Leo in her life. Did she just keep doing what she'd been doing? Letting happen what was going to happen seemed to be working out just fine. Perhaps that was all there was to it?

She yawned again. Lordy, she hoped she didn't fall asleep on the guy later. Tonight, when he visited, she was going to take a chance and bare her heart like never before. Like everything depended on it. In a sense it did. He was her everything.

Instead of that sounding corny, it sounded right. Truthful.

The phone rang. That sounded like work.

She snorted at her poor joke, and because Fiona had a last-minute walk-in in her chair, Kaydee walked over to the desk and answered the phone. Someone called to schedule a cut and color for next week. She wrote it the book and frowned when she took note of the date.

Alarm bells went off in her head.

Trying not to panic, she walked as calmly as possible to the office to retrieve her pocket calendar from her purse. She was probably mistaken. Life was a bit crazy, what with all the showings, and working on the house, and here at the salon, and seeing Leo. All of which was great. She probably had the wrong date stuck in her head. The wrong week.

Opening the bottom drawer in the desk, she bit her lower lip and reached past Fiona's purse to yank hers out. Yeah. She was forever remembering the wrong week, hence the reason she always marked a big X on the day of her period.

Instead of digging in her purse, Kaydee turned it upside down and dumped the contents on the desk. Her hand was shaking too much to bother with fishing for it. Inhaling slow and steady…twice, she reached for the small calendar, flipped to last month, and gasped.

Of all times not to be wrong…

Still staring at the calendar, she sank into the chair behind the desk and blinked. Maybe she had today's date wrong. No. She recounted the weeks since X day.

Shit.

Has it been that long? She'd lost track. Hadn't even realized she was late. She was never late. Ever.

"Hey, Kaydee, last client left, so I locked the door. Are you…" Her friend's voice trailed off. She must've seen the panic on Kaydee's face, because she rushed close to peer at what she was clutching.

The pocket calendar.

Realization entered Fi's eyes and lifted her brow. "Are you?" she asked in a hushed tone, despite the fact that she'd just stated the customers were gone.

Remembering to breathe, she lifted a shoulder. "I don't know. Maybe? I-I'm a little late."

"How late?"

"Four days. But I can't be…you know." She shot to her feet and began to pace, refusing to say the other *P* word. That might make it happen. She wasn't taking any chances. "I mean, we never even had unprotected sex, Fi. So I can't be. It's probably just the stress or something." Yeah, she stopped pacing. That had to be it. "I read somewhere that stress could affect a cycle."

Her friend put a hand on her shoulder, and her expression softened. "Kay, so could a defective condom. It's as good as unprotected."

Shoot. Not what she wanted to hear.

"But you're right," Fi said, squeezing her shoulder, the gleam in her eyes much more positive than before. "There are a lot of factors that could throw off your cycle."

Yeah. Like a baby.

She closed her eyes and sucked in a breath. The last thing Leo needed right now was a baby. Life was finally going good for the guy. He was taking chances—she was proof. So was their relationship. Yeah…she and Leo had a relationship, even though nothing was ever stated. And he was reaching for a goal now. Looking toward the future instead of living hour to hour. Day to day.

Just last Sunday, he told her everything about his plans to invest in At-Ease Ranch, after he saved up a certain amount. Kaydee was so damn proud of him. Even told him, but he'd brushed it off, then brushed her mouth—with his; of course, that caused her mind to fog and need to take over.

But before the mind-fogging incident, she'd been touched beyond anything that he'd confided his At-Ease plans to her. And not during sex, or even afterward, when their defenses were always down. No. It'd been while they were eating dinner. *Dinner.* That had made a much bigger impact on her.

Still did.

"Tell you what," Fiona said, dipping down to catch her gaze. "Since we're done with work, how about we stop by the store and grab a test?"

A test. Yeah. She should probably do that. Drawing in a breath, she began to shove everything back into her purse. "Okay. No sense in worrying about anything until I know for sure."

But she knew. She'd never been late in her life.

An hour later, she stood next to Fiona in her bathroom—the one she remodeled with Leo. The one they made beautiful. The one they probably made a baby in.

At least, if the three sticks they stared at on the counter were correct. All three pregnancy tests sported double pink lines in their digital windows. A positive result.

Kaydee was pregnant.

Her heart rocked, and her queasy stomach felt…well, queasy.

"No wonder I've been so tired this week," she said, then promptly yawned.

Fi tipped her head. "Are you going to keep it?"

"Yes," she said with a jerk of her head, while her hand automatically covered her belly. "I'd never give up my baby."

My baby…

God, Kaydee really thought once she got confirmation that she'd freak out. Shed a few tears. Curl up in bed. Funny thing was, she suddenly felt grounded. It was weird. But in a good way. Like she had a purpose. Someone to love whom she wouldn't have to leave, and who wouldn't leave her…at least, not until college.

She hoped.

"Are you going to tell Leo?"

Her euphoria evaporated. "Yes. Of course." She'd never keep it from him.

But how would he take it?

He never made her any promises to stick around. Heck, they hadn't even really labeled their relationship as a relationship, although she considered it one. A great one. Did he? And she had no idea how he felt about having children.

She sighed, and it quickly turned into a yawn, right before her phone vibrated with a text in her pocket. Her heart skipped a beat, then raced when she saw it was Leo. Was he here already?

Can't stay tonight. Have to turn and burn after dinner with Gram. Sorry.

Disappointment mixed with relief. Telling him about the baby was going to change things between them. Big-time. No matter his response. And she knew there was a huge chance it wouldn't be a good one.

She also knew something was off. Knew it in her gut. Maybe the baby was increasing her intuition. Maybe it was just because she was so in tune with Leo. Whatever the case, Kaydee was getting a weird vibe.

Okay. Everything all right?

She responded and hit send. Then she walked out of the bathroom and straight to the window in her front bedroom to glance across at Ava's. Leo was just getting out of his truck. He glanced at her house, took a step, then stopped.

Her heart squeezed. That wasn't good. It was as if he was afraid to come over. But why?

She glanced at her phone. No response yet. Careful to stay out of view, she stood there watching as indecision rooted him to his grandmother's driveway. She thought briefly about texting him again, but what would she say? What could she say? It wasn't like she was going to bring up the baby tonight. Hell no. Not if he was already wrestling with something.

A second later, he straightened his shoulders and started to cross the street toward her house. She let out a breath she hadn't realized she was holding and rushed out into the hallway. "Fi, Leo's on his way over. Could you do me a favor and stay up here? Something's up, but I don't know if I can get him to tell me. He isn't staying long. He has to go back to Joyful."

"Okay," Fi said. "No baby talk?"

She shook her head. "No. Not tonight." Then she turned and headed downstairs as the doorbell echoed through the house.

That was going to be a tricky subject. One she wasn't even ready to broach. Besides, all she'd done was pee on a stick. Three of them. Maybe it was better to see a doctor first and get professional confirmation before upsetting the apple cart.

Feeling a little better, she put a smile on her face and opened the door.

Chapter Eighteen

For the past hour, Leo wrestled with the question of whether to see Kaydee or not when he came up here to his grandmother's. And once he arrived he fought against his urge to flee. The damn reflex was ingrained in him, deeper, stronger than he'd realized. He thought he'd buried it, along with his drinking and his demons, but the second shit started to fall apart at work today, it resurfaced.

But his feelings for Kaydee were stronger and won out.

For how long?

Before he could form an answer, her door opened, and she was standing in front of him, looking happy and beautiful... and anxious.

God, he hated that he was the dark to her light.

It was her light that reached him, and he felt as if everything inside him took a breath. A deep one.

"Hi." Color rose into her face, and damn, he didn't think he'd ever get tired of watching it happen.

"Hey," he said, then, because he needed to touch her—needed their connection more than air—he stepped right up to her and pulled her in for kiss.

With a sigh, she opened up for him and pressed close. There she went with her unequivocal, unquestioning acceptance again. She didn't stop him. Didn't ask questions. Just gave and gave.

And God, he needed that right now. Needed to feel wanted. Needed her.

But was it really fair to Kaydee?

That damn question again. All day it'd reverberated in his head like a broken record. From the start, he knew she was too good for him. It was the reason he hadn't acted on his attraction to her for so long. She deserved the best in life.

Dammit. He wanted to be that for her. He just wasn't sure if he was.

With another sigh, she broke the kiss to press small ones along his jaw, half on, half off his lips. God, she was sweet. So damn sweet. He ran his hands up and down her back, closing his eyes as he let that sweetness wash over him, almost making him whole.

Almost.

He was in his own way.

How could he possibly tell her he loved her and mean it if he chose to be selfish and put himself first instead of thinking about what was best for her? Was he really the best choice for her? Someone tainted and damaged? Someone who attracted trouble without effort?

Did he really want to wait around until he soured her carefree ways?

No. He didn't want that to happen, and yet he didn't want to leave her, either. Christ. Wasn't there an option that kept her unhurt and in his life? That was the option he wanted.

God…he wanted it bad.

"You okay?" she asked, her hand warm on his face.

He blinked his eyes open and frowned. He hadn't

realized she'd been watching him. Damn. Exactly what had she seen? And it didn't matter that he'd had his eyes closed. The woman saw through every last one of his barriers, past each of his layers, right into what was left of his heart and soul.

"Yeah." He blew out a breath. "Just a long day at work."

She stepped back but held on to his arm. "Do you want to come in?"

Hell yeah. So bad.

"No." He shook his head, trying to keep her welfare first. "Can't. Gram's expecting me for dinner, then I have to get back to the ranch."

Not really. There wasn't anything pressing going on there. No. The problem was here. He needed to keep his distance from her. At least until he figured his shit out.

Concern darkened her eyes. "Is everything okay there?"

"Yeah," he lied through his teeth, although technically, the ranch *was* fine. Work was the problem.

"You sure?" She stepped back out onto the porch, right in front of him again, and cupped his face. "What aren't you telling me? Maybe I can help?"

Blame it on exhaustion, or his need to bask in the warmth of her gaze, or maybe it was because she had superpowers and sucked the smart from his brain. Because before he knew it, he opened up and gave her a brief overview about the countertop, only telling her the wrong one was delivered. Of course, he left out the part about him being bad luck, and that he was considering resigning his supervisory position after the job was done.

"That's terrible, Leo." A deep frown marred her brow. "I'm sorry."

He stiffened. Not as sorry as him. But he was going to clean up his own mess. Stone did enough of that shit for him in the past. No more.

The exhaustion he felt suddenly appeared in her eyes, and she yawned. Twice.

"Sorry," she mumbled through the smile she covered with her hand.

He smiled, too. "It's okay," he said, lightly grasping her upper arms as he pressed his lips to her forehead. "Go back inside. I have to get going, anyway."

Regret and something he couldn't quite read flashed through her eyes until she blinked, then only warmth remained. "Okay. I guess I'll see you on Friday."

This time regret flickered through him. He shook his head and told her about Tucker and the group therapy session.

"Hey, don't apologize for helping someone." She set a palm on his chest. "I think that's great. And that you're amazing."

Christ. He didn't feel amazing…except where her palm covered his heart…the one she owned. And because it felt so damn good, he grasped that hand, brought her palm to his lips, then kissed it before releasing her. "No. That'd be you. You're the amazing one."

She chuckled. "Then let's agree to disagree."

"Okay." Without much thought, he laughed, too.

"Don't worry about your grandmother on Friday," she said. "I'll take her to bingo with my grandfather. You know they like to ride together anyway."

He blew out a breath. "Thanks." Then gave her another quick kiss on the forehead, because if he went anywhere near her mouth again, not only was he going inside, he'd never leave. "Good night, Kaydee," he said, before turning her around and gently pushing her into the house.

"Good night," she mumbled through another yawn.

He waited until she shut the door, then headed across the street. Seeing her was probably a mistake, but right now, he didn't care. He needed it. Needed to see her. Needed to not hurt her today. He still wasn't sure about the future.

Even though he'd had a shit day, he entered his grandmother's house with a pleasant expression on his face. Even managed to eat and hold a normal conversation with her, too.

Of course, she was way too sharp for his own good, and called him out on. "Don't do it."

"Do what?"

"Walk away from that sweet girl."

Jesus. How the hell had she figured that out? His Ranger face must be slipping. No sense in denying it. "I'm toxic." He exhaled. "I don't want to bring her down."

"You're in love with her, aren't you?"

"Doesn't matter."

She slapped the table. "Bullshit."

His lips twitched. She had spunk.

"It matters the most," she said in a calm, firm voice. "So answer me."

He blew out a breath and sat back. "Yes, I love her. That's why I should probably walk away. To give her a chance at a good life."

"Leo." She cocked her head, and her incredulous gaze bored deep. "What makes you think she wouldn't have a good life with you?"

His guilt made him feel unclean. Unworthy, and although he knew Kaydee would never agree with that, he wasn't going to give her a chance to. "She deserves someone without my kind of past. Someone strong, not weak. Someone like her who's righteous and helps others."

"But Leo, don't you see? You *are* all those things."

He laughed without amusement and shot to his feet. "Come on, Gram. A guy who takes a handful of pills and washes them down with a bottle of whiskey is not righteous or helping others."

Guilt flooded his stomach in a nauseous swirl. Unable to face her, he turned around and strode to the sink, trying to focus on something...anything outside. But all he saw were the faces of his family and friends when he'd come to in the hospital after he'd been unconscious for several days.

Worry. Exhaustion. Anger. Guilt. You name it, he saw it darkening their eyes. Aging their faces. He'd put everyone through hell. And it was his fault. His fucking selfish fault.

But he wasn't that guy anymore, his mind interjected. He'd moved past all that. He'd learned from it. Grew from it. He was out of those woods.

But barely. What if something bad happened? He knew how far he could fall. Christ, the last thing he wanted was to drag Kaydee down with him.

"We all have things in our past we're not proud of, Leo," she said from behind him. "No one is exempt from that. But if you learn from it and grow, then you need to cut yourself a break and move on." He felt her palm on his back. "I'm damn proud of you and all you've accomplished. We all are." She moved her hand to his shoulder and squeezed. "Maybe you're looking at your past all wrong."

He grunted. "Only one way *to* look at it. I brought others down. Without trying."

He'd been a burden. Not before Drew's death, but since? Hell yeah. He'd been a piece of shit burden and fucking hated the fact. Hated that he lived in a house his buddies co-owned, but he didn't. Worked for a company his buddies co-owned, but he didn't, although he was changing all that now. It made him feel like he was less trouble...less of a mooch.

But what really bothered him—what he could *never* fix— was the fact that he'd let the images in his head eat at him until only turning to booze had made sense.

He'd been an idiot *and* a burden. No way would he let that happen again.

But it didn't guarantee that he wouldn't hurt Kaydee.

"You're definitely looking at this wrong, Leo," she said with another squeeze to his shoulder. "You're a gift."

He snorted and turned to face her. "Now who's slinging bullshit?"

She lifted her hand to pat his face. "Sometimes someone needs to fall in order to lift others up."

He stiffened as her words sank in. That would mean he inspired. Now that was bullshit. The last thing he felt was inspiring.

Since he had nothing to say to that, he shook his head and left.

. . .

Friday came and went with not much communication with Leo. He sent Kaydee a few texts…mainly in response to hers. It did little to alleviate that bad vibe that had poured off him on Wednesday.

A call from Jovy yesterday had sent her heart into her throat. She'd wanted desperately to ask about Leo but didn't. The woman had asked if she and Fiona were free tomorrow to come to At-Ease to do a hair-cutting clinic for the veterans. She'd kept the conversation about what she and Fiona would need.

What Kaydee needed was Leo.

A tiny flicker of hope fluttered through her chest. If she didn't see him today, maybe she'd at least run into him at his ranch tomorrow. It was already Saturday afternoon now, and she still hadn't heard from him. Not a word or a text. Nothing. The sick feeling in her stomach increased. And it had nothing to do with the baby.

Their baby…

She'd made an appointment with the doctor next week.

No one else knew about the baby except Fiona. But she wanted to tell Leo. Needed to tell him.

God. What if he didn't want the baby? Didn't want her?

Kaydee's stomach lurched. She rushed into her bathroom to throw up. When finished, she rose to her feet and placed a hand on her belly. "I know, sweetheart. Life without Daddy in it is a sickening thought."

Whatever was wrong, she'd fix it. She had to. Over the past few days, she'd come to terms with several things, and not just the "having a baby" part. The "I love Leo" part, too. She did love him. It was clear now, and never more so than at the thought of not having him in her life. That put it all into perspective.

So, yeah, she needed to see him. To talk to him. Just be with him. Things were better when they were together. Like Wednesday. Something was wrong, and he hadn't stayed long, but he'd wanted to. She could see it in his eyes. Feel it in his touch.

Need. Longing…love. Yes, she'd seen that, too.

All those emotions had deepened his gaze. They were all there, along with one she hated to see.

Torment.

But why? And what caused it?

She hadn't even mentioned the baby, so it couldn't have been that. And just a simple mix-up with the wrong countertop wouldn't do it. There had to be more. But she couldn't get him to tell her, especially if they weren't talking.

Sighing, she headed downstairs, debating what to do about her cellar steps. They'd never finished repairing them. The final three were already cut, but still needed to be screwed into place on the new risers Leo had built. Something she could handle…if she had a drill.

Maybe she should buy one.

Risers weren't the only thing Leo had created down

there. The talented man had built up a deep, fierce, blazing tide inside her that'd crashed onto an erotic shore she longed to revisit. Yeah, they kind of got sidetracked with sexytimes.

Totally his fault.

Looking all badass and hot with his tool belt slung low on his hips, biceps flexing under his T-shirt, back muscles rippling, giving her naughty, needy thoughts… The sight of him made her crazy and hungry and wanton, and she sort of attacked him. In a good way. He didn't complain. No. He embraced it and her, whispering sexy, dirty, delicious promises in her ear as he made good on each and every one of them.

Great. Now she was hot and bothered. And alone. She'd never felt so alone.

The doorbell rang, and the sudden sound jarred her. She jumped and placed a hand over her racing heart as hope flickered through her chest.

Leo?

On the way to the door, she dug out her phone, noting no missed calls or text. She sighed. She doubted he'd just show up. A look out the peephole had her sucking in a breath. Wrong.

Reining in her pulse, she shoved her phone in her pocket and opened the door.

Shoulder against the frame, one hand gripping his toolbox, the other shoved deep in his pocket, Leo didn't say anything, or move, except to lift his head and meet her gaze. Her indrawn breath echoed between them. His eyes were dull, clouded, and his mouth was tight…grim.

"Are you… okay?" she asked. A feeling of déjà vu from the other night rippled through her. "What's wrong?"

He gave one slow shake of his head. "I've come to finish your stairs. Is that okay?"

She frowned. "Yes. Of course." Then moved aside to let him in, wanting desperately to lean close and kiss him, but he was so rigid.

He stepped inside, his mouth twitching slightly, no doubt at her appearance. She was wearing cutoffs and her Captain America T-shirt. The irony of the fact that that character was best friends with the character he resembled wasn't lost on her.

She smiled. It was the reason she'd bought it.

"Fitting," he said, but there was something off in his voice. His gaze was still dull, too. Then he muttered under his breath about light and dark. "I'm gonna finish those steps."

"Okay," she said again. "Need help?"

"No." He shook his head. "I can handle it. Won't take long," he said, and without meeting her gaze, he disappeared downstairs.

While he worked, she paced in her kitchen, right near the cellar door, stressed and worried over the reason for his bleak look. He was trying to shut her out. It was painfully obvious. She needed to reach him. Get rid of the clouds. Tell him how she felt. Tell him about the baby.

The sound of his footsteps on the stairs ten minutes later halted her pacing. But not her worry. Or her determination. They needed to talk.

"Done," he announced, still not meeting her gaze.

Dammit.

Careful of the toolbox he gripped tight, she stepped close and curved her palm around his rough jaw, forcing him to look at her. "What is going on?"

His expression was…not there. Lacking. Blank. Like he refused to feel. Refused to let anyone in. Even her. Or maybe especially her.

Like maybe she'd gotten to him and he didn't want her to…

Kaydee swallowed past the lump in her throat and tried again. "Leo, talk to me. What's wrong?"

Her heart ached, not for herself, but for him. A man

who'd broken through her walls, stripped away her shield, and made her want a long-term relationship, made her open up and feel. Deeply. For him. And she did. So very much.

"Let me help," she said. "Let me in." The muscles in his jaw rippled under her hand as if he was clenching his teeth. She lifted her free hand and placed it over his heart. "Whatever this is, we're in it together. Learning to open up, commit, give, take." She almost said "love" but didn't want to overload him with too much, too soon. "And I happen to like what this is, and I know you do, too."

Instead of denying it or pushing her away, he kicked one of her kitchen chairs out and put his toolbox down, then put his hands on her hips and backed her up until she hit the counter behind her.

"Leo," she said breathlessly.

He shook his head, planted his hands on the counter on either side of her, caging her in, then leaned close and covered her mouth with his, as if he couldn't help himself. She sighed. It felt so damn good to touch him, embrace him…and she did, sliding her hands up around his neck to hold the back of his head while he plundered.

The kiss was different than his other ones. He left out the teasing, tasting, and warm-up. This was all raw need and desperation. It felt more real than any kiss she'd ever experienced in her life.

But something was wrong. His whole body was tension-filled. Not all of it in a good way. The muscles in his neck were rock hard, knotted, and he was warm, almost too hot. And when he broke the kiss, he closed his eyes. "I shouldn't be here. And I sure as hell shouldn't have done that."

Chapter Nineteen

"Why?" Kaydee touched Leo's face again. It seemed to be the only damn way to get him to look at her. His eyes opened, and she found his gaze stormy. Troubled. Her heart lurched. "Did I do something?"

"What?" His brows crashed together. "No. Absolutely not. You're great. Sweet. Honest. Perfect. I'm the one who's..." His voice trailed off, and he pushed away to turn his back on her.

Something deep within her quivered.

And she didn't feel like she was any of those things. "No one is perfect, Leo. I'm far from it." She moved close to place a hand on his back. "And I really wish you'd tell me what's wrong."

"Bad week."

Something more was going on. She could feel it. "Is there anything I can do?"

"No." He moved out from under her touch. "I don't want to draw you into my mess."

Dammit. She was right. Something was going on.

"If there's one thing I've learned over the years," she said, stepping around to face him, "it's that problems are easier solved when shared. I've learned that the hard way."

She smiled, but he shook his head.

"Forget it. It's not your problem and I'm not sharing." He strode to the chair and grabbed his toolbox. "You deserve better," he said, and turned toward the doorway.

She shot in front of him and pressed her palm on his chest. "*You* are better for me, Leo. You taught me to open up. That it's okay to make connections. To live a little. Take chances. I took one on you, and I'm glad I did. So glad." All of a sudden, emotions swirled inside her and closed her throat, cutting off her profession of love.

"Yeah, well, you shouldn't," he growled. "I'm toxic, Kaydee. I'll end up letting you down. I let people down. It's what I do. I don't want to. Hell, I certainly don't plan to, but it's only a matter of time."

She shook her head, feeling his heartbeat strong and hard under her palm. "I don't believe you will."

"Believe me. I have a history of it. Stone. The rest of the guys. My mom. Grandmother. Drew. That little gi—" He paused to swallow. "I've let them all down. What if I add you to that list? God, I don't want to. I refuse to."

"You won't."

He backed up a few steps as if he couldn't bear for her to touch him. "There are things you don't know about me. Bad things. Things I'm goddamned ashamed of."

Her heart broke at the desolation and guilt rough in his voice. He was talking about his hospitalization. "I *do* know about it," she told him quietly. "I've known since the first week we met that you tried to silence the horror in your head with a bunch of pills and booze."

His face paled, and his gaze seemed even more hollow. "You know? How?"

"The rec center," she said. "I overheard you talking to someone during one of the sit-in therapy sessions. I didn't mean to eavesdrop—I was outside the room waiting for my grandfather to get out of bingo down the hall and...yeah."

"You've known this whole time?"

"Yes."

He blinked. "And you still wanted to be around me?"

"Of course." She balked. "Jesus, don't you see? Your past—good and bad—has shaped you into the person you are today. And I really, *really* like who you are, Leo. I like being with you. And I like who I am when I'm with you."

"I really like you, too, Kaydee," he said, and his words would've warmed her heart if it weren't for his cold, hard gaze. "And I refuse to bring you down if I relapse or something. You deserve better."

"No. I deserve *you*."

He shook his head. "You deserve someone you can count on. Someone who makes you happy and isn't a burden."

She smiled. "You've just described yourself, Leo, because *you* are all those things to me. And more."

He muttered a curse. "You're not listening to me. I told you, I'm toxic. I unintentionally hurt the people I care about."

"The only way you could hurt me is by shutting me out."

His chin lifted. "Maybe it's for the better."

She frowned. "Better? For who? You?" Her heart slammed into her ribs, and she waved her hand at him. "Because it sure as hell isn't better for me. Or our baby."

Dammit. She hadn't meant to blurt it out like that.

His head jerked back, then his whole body stilled. "Baby?"

Inhaling deep, she cursed her stupidity and nodded. "Yes. I'm pregnant."

"Pregnant..." He dropped his toolbox back on the chair, shoved a hand through his hair, and held the back of his neck as he blew out a breath. A long one, then he blinked and straightened before his set his focus on her. "How are you feeling?"

Warmth broke through the chill that settled over her chest. How could he not see how much he really did care about her?

"Tired and a little queasy, but otherwise, I'm okay."

He nodded but remained silent, stunned expression still glued to his face.

She folded her arms across her chest to keep from reaching out to touch him. "This isn't how I wanted to tell you. I'm sorry. But it feels like you're about to walk out on me and I thought you should know."

Again, he nodded but remained silent. God...he really was about to walk out.

The chill returned to her body with such force and so fast her chest felt like it had caved in on itself.

Somehow, she managed to find her voice. "Look, the last thing I want is for you to feel obligated to stay with me now."

As he opened his mouth to respond, his phone rang. "Sorry," he told her before taking the call. "All right. No problem. I'll head back in a few minutes." He shoved his phone in his pocket and turned to face her. "That was Stone. They're calling an emergency meeting. I need to get back to the ranch."

She held her disappointment in check. "Of course. We can talk about this when you come back." Desperate move. She knew but didn't care. Just hoped he'd come back.

God, how she hoped.

Another silent nod from him tightened the invisible grip on her heart. She watched him lift his toolbox, hoping he'd say something positive or comforting, but when he straightened, his expression was still dialed to somber. This time when he made to leave the kitchen and head for the front door, she didn't stop him.

But she couldn't bear to let him leave without trying to reach him one last time. "I have my first doctor's appointment. Nine a.m. on Tuesday."

He halted with his hand on the knob but didn't turn around.

"It'd be nice if you were there," she said, blinking away the tears gathering in her eyes, willing him to turn so she could see his face.

But he didn't. Just dipped his head once in acknowledgment, then walked out of her house.

Maybe her life.

Chapter Twenty

Baby…

Kaydee was carrying his baby. And knew about his past. She *knew*. All this time, she knew…

Leo didn't exactly remember walking out of her house, but when he blinked, he was across the street on his grandmother's porch. He'd gone numb. So numb, he'd crossed a street without realizing it.

How fucked up was that?

After telling his grandmother he was heading back to Joyful, he climbed in his truck and stared out the windshield. *A baby…* Before backing out of the driveway, he slapped his face a few times to clear the fog from his brain. Didn't need to drive numb. He'd already hurt enough people in his life.

The last thing he wanted to do was add Kaydee and their baby to that list, but no matter what he did at this point, she was destined to top it. Wasn't she better off if he bowed out from the start than for him to leave when she needed him most?

Like now? his mind chimed in. She was pregnant. So

didn't right now qualify as one of those times?

Why the hell did he keep questioning himself about leaving her? That was something the Leo from two years ago would do. He wasn't that person anymore.

Was he?

He muttered a curse and gripped the steering wheel. All during his drive, he tried to get his brain to accept the bombs she'd dropped, and his mind to tell him what his options were. He was still looking for the one where he got to keep her without hurting her. But it wasn't even about them now.

It was about the baby.

An unexpected fierce protectiveness surged through him. He was going to be a dad.

But he wasn't good father material. Maybe he should protect the child from himself.

And that was as far as he got in his head before he pulled up in front of the ranch, noting Cord parking his truck. Stone had been serious about calling a full meeting. Had to be if Cord was here on a Saturday and not on his own ranch with Haley. It was already heading into evening.

Leo slid from his truck and wondered briefly what could be so important to have them put their private lives on hold to get together on a day off…then promptly shook his head. Didn't matter. He was grateful as hell that Stone had called. Gave him an out with Kaydee. Saved his ass, because she'd been wearing him down, making him want what she was pitching. Need what she wanted to give him.

And that was selfish as hell of him.

"Hey," Cord said, falling into step with him. "You look like shit."

He snorted. "Good to see you too, Warlock."

Cord's lips twitched as they entered the house.

"In here," Stone called out from the office.

Leo preceded Cord through the doorway. Blame it on

the concussions he was still suffering from the bombs Kaydee dropped, or the fact that he was too caught up in his shit to notice the guys flanking him.

Until it was too late.

The door closed, and he heard the lock *click* into place. That was his *aha* moment. Leo stiffened, and a sense of dread filled him.

Christ. He stilled and turned to see Cord lean against the door with his arms folded across his chest. He shot his gaze to Stone, Vince, and Brick—standing, not sitting—all regarding him with concern pinching their faces.

Ah...fuck.

"Seriously? An intervention?" He ground his teeth, suddenly wishing he'd stayed in Dallas.

The last time he was in the hospital—more than a year ago for alcohol poisoning—he swore to himself he was never going to give his friends a reason to look at him that way ever again. The looks haunted him ever since. And he hadn't given them cause...until today.

His stomach clenched. "What did I do?"

Was it Blanche? Had she told them about the mix-up? He'd left her with a completed kitchen that morning. She'd been thrilled, even signed off on it. He'd filed the paperwork before leaving for Dallas.

Brick cocked his head. "You tell us."

"Gonna need you to be clearer than that," he said, leaning against the desk, keeping the door in his peripheral vision in case Cord left his post.

Snow would fall in hell first.

"Kaydee," Stone said, stepping close to put a hand on his shoulder. "What happened between you two this week?"

How the hell...? No way would she have called. The woman was still too private, too closed off to the ways of sharing with well-meaning, meddling friends.

Stone's lips twitched. "Your grandmother called me on Wednesday."

Leo closed his eyes, let out a long, ragged breath, and *thunked* his forehead to his closed fist a few times. Then a few more.

"Knock any sense in there yet?" Brick's amused tone had him lifting his head and opening his eyes.

He flipped the idiot off.

Vince snorted. "That'd be a negatory there, Romeo."

He turned his attention back to Stone. "Sorry. Gram shouldn't have bothered you."

Lord knew what she'd told them.

"Bothered?" Vince exhaled loudly. "Leo, you're not a bother. You're a *brother*. We're always going to worry about you."

Stiffening, he straightened from the desk. This was exactly what he *didn't* want. Their worry. Anxiety.

"No more than we would any one of us," Stone added, no doubt reading his thoughts. "You've taken part in several interventions, and none were about you."

"Yeah, they were for each of us," Cord said, still guarding the door.

"Because at some point we had our heads so far up our asses that we needed help prying them lose." Brick grinned. "We're here today to return the favor."

"So, what did you do? Or did we catch you before you did it?" Stone asked.

He blinked at them, wondering what he needed to say and how much to get them to open the damn door.

"You know," Vince said conversationally, "the girls are bingeing a Netflix series, so we've got all night."

He muttered a curse. They weren't going to stop until he fucking talked. Fine. "I'm in love with Kaydee."

Brick exchanged a look with Vince. Cord blinked, and

Stone grinned. Leo ignored them. He chose to tip his head back and stare at the ceiling fan, trying to count the paddles as they spun around, making him dizzy as shit but he didn't care. He said all that mattered.

"And?"

Of course it would be Stone who prompted for more. Mother hen of the group. Always trying to fix everyone.

Thank God.

They were lucky to have him. *He* was lucky to have him. But right now, Leo didn't want fixing.

"*And* I don't want to hurt her," he said with a clenched jaw.

"So you didn't fuck things up with her then?" Brick asked.

Leo transferred his gaze from the ceiling fan to the guy and found him now kicked back on the couch that lined the wall opposite of Warlock's post.

"What my brother means is, did you walk out on Kaydee or not?" Stone asked, his wording no less painful to hear.

He lifted a shoulder. "Jury's still out. We were kind of in the middle of it when I got your summoning."

Vince and Stone both muttered curses. Brick sat up.

But Cord? He just stared at him. And stared. "You're running. Scared."

Growling, he turned to face the guy. "Let me the fuck out."

"Not yet," Cord said, eyebrow raised in silent question as if to ask whether Leo really wanted to take him on.

Maybe. He'd either get out or dead. Either way, this damn interrogation would end.

"Okay, so you love Kaydee," Stone said, regaining his attention. "And don't want to hurt her. What else? Come on, Leo. I know there are a few more ands and a but in there, too. Might as well spill it. Cord's not moving until you do."

Shit. He met Stone's gaze. "And I don't want to pull her into my vortex of disappointment. I let everyone down, I'll eventually let her down, too. Maybe even *drag* her down."

Brick grumbled. "Bullshit."

"You don't know that," Vince said.

"Vince is right." Cord cocked his head. "No one's perfect."

"Kaydee's damn close," he said without thinking.

Stone leaned next to him against the desk. "You need to fix it with her. She's good for you."

"The past few weeks, you've been happy," Vince said. "Truly happy. You've laughed and smiled, and Emma said she even heard you whistle. She *cried*. You brought tears to my fiancée's eyes. Happy tears."

He didn't know how to respond to that, so he didn't. Just stood there, locked in a room by his old Ranger unit, who waited for him to come to some sort of a realization. Of what? He had no fucking clue.

So he thought about Kaydee and how he felt when he was with her. Like a superhero. Like he could accomplish anything. Like a normal, upstanding man. She made him feel happy and good. Good to be alive. With her he wasn't the guy with a bad past, or unreliable, or unlovable. He'd always thought she made him feel those things because she hadn't known about his past. But she had…

With her, he was capable, accepted, needed…loved. He sucked in a breath on that one.

"Ah…think he's getting it," Brick said.

Leo ignored him on the outside, but on the inside, he agreed with the goof. He *was* getting it. Finally. "I'm an asshole. A scared one."

"Welcome to the club." Stone chuckled.

Kaydee had known about his moments of weakness, his mistakes, his trials and tribulations…and loved him anyway.

She'd never said the words, but he'd seen them in her adoring gaze, felt them in her tender touch. She still saw something good in him. The good he wanted the world to see, instead of the mistakes of his past. She got it. She got him. Always had.

The restless spirit took a chance on him, despite her ingrained safeguarding. She didn't open up so easily. He understood her. He'd been around a few army brats. Like Kaydee, some grew numb from all the moving, figured why bother to open up, and eventually adopted a vagabond lifestyle in adulthood. Kaydee didn't let too many people close because she drifted. But she'd opened up to him. He was one of the lucky ones she let in, and when she had, she gave everything. Held nothing back.

And he repaid that by walking out.

He shook his head. "I'm a fucking *asshole*."

Cord grinned. "Think we've already established that."

Stone started coughing to hide a laugh. Vince and Brick didn't bother to hide a damn thing.

Before her, he'd been existing, fooling himself into thinking he was living and experiencing life, moving forward, planning a future. But none of that got his blood pumping or heart racing or body aching like a simple glance from Kaydee.

She did it for him. Without her, he only skated through life.

He didn't want to skate anymore. Or just exist. He wanted to fly. With his superwoman.

And right now, he wished he could kick his own ass.

"So, are you ready to let Kaydee fully into your life?" Brick asked.

Vince cocked his head. "And not worry about your past?"

"It's done," Stone said. "Over. Time to move on."

He blew out a long breath and rubbed his temple. "If she'll have me." He had to make up for walking out with only a half nod and no words…she deserved the words. Deserved the world.

"She will." Stone placed a hand on his shoulder. "We've seen the way she looks at you like you hung the moon. She's crazy about you."

He met his buddy's gaze head-on. "She's also pregnant."

The room grew silent. No one moved. No one blinked. Just stared at him with their mouths stuck open.

Stone was the first to recover. He blinked, then squeezed his shoulder. "Congratulations, man. That's terrific."

Then Leo went through one backslapping handshake after another. Starting with Brick, followed by Vince. Then the door guard, who finally left his perch.

"It is a good thing, right?" Cord asked. "You okay with being a dad?"

Every damn emotion in the alphabet hit Leo at once. After a few stuttered heartbeats, he finally nodded, then shoved a hand through his hair. "What if I suck at it, though? I don't want to ruin this child's life. Don't want to mess it up."

Stone shook his head. "Again, no one's perfect. Everyone makes mistakes. The fact that you're concerned about it will keep you motivated to do your best. And that's all anyone could ask. I think you're going to make a fantastic father."

"Hell yeah." Vince grinned. "You help so many people."

"I do what you all do. Nothing more." He snorted. "Except screw up. I'm not the type to inspire."

Stone stilled. "Are you serious? Leo, you're the reason half the veterans chose to give At-Ease a chance."

"I am?" His heart stuttered again. "What do you mean? Why?"

"Because you've lived in the shadows where some still dwell. You survived, and now thrive," Stone said. "You give them hope that they can climb out, too. You're living proof it is possible."

Well, hell. Air left his lungs, and it felt like Lula Belle

kicked him in the ribs.

"You get them, and they gravitate toward you," Brick said.

Vince pointed at him. "They get acceptance, not judgment, from you. That's huge. So huge, man."

"Some look up to you," Cord said, and effectively knocked the air from Leo's lungs *again*.

Who the hell would look up to him?

"Like Tucker," Stone said. "He's come to me on several occasions the past two weeks to thank me for putting him on your crew. And I noticed you got him to group therapy yesterday."

The kid even stayed until the end. Leo already promised to go with him again next week.

"I hope you see how you're more than motivational," Vince said. "You're the reason At-Ease is here."

"Because I fucked up," he grumbled.

Stone smiled. "Yeah, and because of that fuckup, how many lives have we changed? Made bearable? *Saved?*"

Emotions swirled in Leo's chest, tightening it to full capacity.

"There are times things happen in life for a reason," Cord said, and it immediately reminded Leo of his grandmother's words.

"Gram said something similar the other day." He gave a half smile. "Sometimes someone needs to fall in order to lift others up."

But there'd be no more falling back into his pit of self-pity and despair. That pit was gone. It was time to grow. To rid himself of those damn demons. To kill off the person he was before. It was time to let go. Time to say goodbye to the broken man—the part of his psyche that always held him down—and embrace the man he had become because of his history. The whole man who acknowledged his past, both dark and light, and moved on. The man Kaydee always saw. The man Kaydee…and their baby deserved.

By putting that old part of himself to rest, Leo felt stronger. Calmer. Like a wiser, better version of himself.

Brick leaned forward. "Damn. I love your Gram."

"Like it or not, Leo," Stone said, "you are the savior of At-Ease."

Savior…

He may be wiser, but he was no one's savior. He was just a guy.

"You've saved people while on active duty and you continue to save them now. You're going to make a hell of a dad." Vince slapped his back. "Emma and the girls are going to flip when they find out about the baby."

He was still trying to process the *savior* and *saving lives* thing, but the instant Vince mentioned Leo was going to be a dad, warmth shot through his body and straightened his spine.

"As long as Beth doesn't want one of her own." Brick shivered. "Our wedding is rushing close. I'd like to survive that first."

Stone laughed. "You're going to do fine. There's nothing to it. Cord and I made it through without a scratch."

"Yep," Cord said. "Just agree to anything my sister wants and you're golden."

Vince turned to him. "Now, how can we help you with Kaydee?"

He inhaled and thought for a moment. The image of her face as he left her kitchen flashed through his mind. The hurt he was trying to shield her from was blatant in the arms crossed over her stomach and her watery eyes. His own stomach clenched hard. She'd been holding back tears… holding *herself* as if hugging would keep it all in.

He needed to fix it. Make up for it. Jesus, he owed her so

much. He owed her everything. "I need to go back there and grovel."

"Chocolates are good," Brick said. "Beth can eat my weight in them."

Momentarily pulled out of his misery, Leo snorted at the analogy. "You're right. I've seen her devour one of Emma's cakes in under a minute. Without coming up for air."

"Roses," Stone said. "Jovy loves them."

"Do you have the tile-cutting saw?" Cord asked.

Brick turned to look at his buddy like his brains were oozing out of his ears. "Saw? Jesus, Cord. Really? Some romantic you are. I feel sorry for Haley on Valentine's Day. You probably buy her kitchen appliances. Or weight-loss DVDs."

Leo snorted again, next to a chuckling Stone.

"I wasn't suggesting it as a gift for Kaydee," Cord said with an eye roll. "You all seem to have that covered. I was asking if he was done with the saw because I need it tomorrow to work on a bathroom at home. It's a surprise for Haley."

"Yeah, I finished with it this morning," Leo said. "It's in the back of my truck."

Brick rose from the couch. "Come on, Cord. I'll help you load it."

"This mean we're done?" He motioned toward the door. "I'm allowed to leave this room."

"Depends." Cord stared at him. "You still think you're unworthy of Kaydee?"

He raised a brow. "Hell yeah. I'll never be worthy of her. She's a saint."

A smile tugged Cord's lips. "Good answer."

"Agreed." Stone slapped a hand on his shoulder and walked with him toward the door. "Let's go brainstorm more groveling ideas."

Chapter Twenty-One

Leo walked with Stone and Vince to the rec room, where the women were binge-watching a show in the far corner. The blind superhero dude again. He smiled at the matching grimaces on his buddies' faces when their women sighed over the shirtless guy on the screen.

"Doesn't even have that much meat on his bones," Vince grumbled, his top lip curling as he looked over at Emma leaning forward in her chair, like Beth, Jovy, and Haley, as if to get close enough to the big-ass TV to lick the screen.

"I know." Stone frowned and shook his head. "Their fascination makes no sense to me."

What fascinated Leo was the fact that the women were so riveted by the show that they tuned everything out, including them. No one even glanced their way.

"No, but it does make for a good night later." Vince waggled his brows, and Leo tried not to throw up in his mouth.

With luck, Leo's good night would include forgiveness from the woman who owned his heart. As soon as he figured out how to make it up to her.

Tension slowly ebbed from his body, and he sank into one of the overstuffed chairs in the middle of the room with a sigh. "So that sucked," he said, closing his eyes. "Glad it's over, though."

"I'm fuckin' proud of you, man," Stone said.

Leo opened his eyes to find his buddy standing in front of him with a beer in each hand and a gray gaze gleaming with pride.

Unsure what to do with the positive emotions flooding his chest, Leo nodded and took the beer Stone offered.

"Yeah. Me, too." Vince grinned.

He shrugged. "Thanks."

Stone cocked his head, and a huge smile ate up his face. "I know I said this earlier, but I'm going to say it again. You're going to make a hell of a dad."

He glanced over at the girls to see if they'd heard, but their attention was still on the screen. Which was a good thing, because all those emotions in Leo's chest backed up into his damn throat and he had to clear it.

"Thanks," he told his buddy again, but apparently it wasn't good enough for Mother Hen. Stone held out his hand, forcing Leo to put his beer down, then stand for a proper backslapping.

"I'm happy for you," Stone said, releasing him so Vince could take over.

"Yeah, me, too," Vince repeated his earlier response through a grin that rivaled Stone's.

He smiled and nodded, but he'd be happier in Dallas.

"Now," Stone began as they all sat down. "As we were saying, what can we do to help you with Kaydee?"

Leo blew out a breath. "No clue."

"It's getting late. Going to head up there tonight?" Vince asked.

He glanced out the siding glass door, noting dusk darkening the sky. Damn. He rubbed the back of his neck. "I wanted to, but by the time I drive up there she'd probably be asleep. I think the baby's making her tired."

"Baby?" Beth's high-pitched, squeaky tone jerked his head back.

"Of course the women would hear that word." Vince grinned. "Now we know what word to use to pull them from their superhero stupor."

"Who's having a baby?" Jovy's overbright gaze shot to him. "You and Kaydee?"

He nodded but had no time to do or say more, because Emma rushed right over, pulled him out of his chair, and hugged him tight. "I'm so happy for you two. Oh my God. This is…oh my God."

Vince chuckled. "Think you covered that already, hun."

Haley hugged him next. "Congratulations."

Jovy followed. "Where is Kaydee?" she asked, glancing around.

"Home," he said, his chest suddenly too tight to say more.

Stone's gaze met his. "Baby's making her tired."

He owed his buddy one for trying to cover up his stupidity. But the women were starting to frown, so questions were eminent.

Haley was the first to call him out. "And you're sitting here and not there…why?"

"Because I'm an ass," he said, just as Cord and Brick walked in.

"Oh, we're at the good part again." Brick grinned and waved at him. "Carry on. Oh, wait. Let me grab a beer and sit down first. I don't want to miss anything."

He wouldn't flip him off with the girls right there. Brick knew it, too. His lips twitched. The bastard.

"So, tell us what's going on," Emma said, sliding her

arm around Vince's waist as the guy dropped his around her shoulders.

"The usual," Vince answered for him with a grin. "He needs to grovel."

Big-time.

Cord came over and hauled Haley's back against his chest, banding his arms around her as he kissed her neck. Then he lifted his head and met Leo's gaze. "Stuffed animal."

"Dude." Brick snorted. "Did you just call your wife a stuffed animal?"

Cord eye-rolled his buddy again and shook his head. "Just a suggestion for the groveling aids."

Leo chuckled. "I'll add it to the list. But it's too late to go up to see her. Or to call. I don't want to wake her, so it looks like I'll have to wait until morning to head to Dallas."

"No need." Jovy shook her head. "Kaydee's coming here tomorrow afternoon to cut hair."

He frowned, not remembering that plan. "She is?"

"Yeah," Jovy said as Stone pulled her down onto his lap. "I talked to her about it on Thursday. Didn't she tell you?"

He shook his head. Kind of hard when they weren't communicating. And they really hadn't said too much this week. His fault. He only stopped in twice. Both times briefly. Just enough time to show his first-class ass act.

"Well, no worries." Emma smiled. "You have tonight and tomorrow morning to practice your groveling skills."

Laughter went up around the room. Funny part was, he was going to need every damn second to prepare.

Chapter Twenty-Two

It was late Sunday afternoon by the time Kaydee finished the last of her haircuts at the ranch. She was kind of proud of herself for keeping it together. Not once, the whole day, had she given in to the tears that sprang up out of nowhere.

Darn out-of-control pregnancy hormones.

She didn't do tears, not since her childhood. That'd cured her of them. Or so she thought. Now she was pregnant and a basket case.

Nuts.

So were her out-of-control feelings for Leo. She reined them in, too. At least, she tried. It was crazy how she'd trekked through most of her life with a tight grip on her emotions, corralling them, allowing only a few select people through the gate. Fi, her parents, her grandfather, Ava, and then she eventually took a chance and let Leo in.

And now she was feeling everything. Too much. And it wasn't the baby. No. This all started the moment she'd met Leo, then escalated when they'd kissed. Ever since their first one, she'd been an emotion receptor or something. They overflowed in her, but it was okay. He made it all good. Made her feel…amazing.

But now…without…

She inhaled and cut that train of thought right off, then did her best to stuff those unwanted emotions back in the caboose. Her time here was up. She could pack up and leave. Maybe without even talking to Leo.

She had mixed emotions about that.

Coming here today, Kaydee had kind of hoped to run into him. Even had a nice fantasy about it. He'd take one look at her, tell her he was sorry, beg her forgiveness, hold her close, and never let her go.

A snort rumbled up her throat but came out as a half sob. Which she promptly covered up with a cough.

Fi glanced over at her. "You okay?"

"Yeah." She lied with a smile. "Just dust or hair or something in my throat."

More like a piece of her broken heart.

Lordy, she really couldn't wait to see the doctor this week. Surely he had some kind of pregnancy emotion supplement or something like that to decrease them. She really had to go nine months like this?

Not going to make it, she thought as she folded her cape and shoved it into her case, along with her scissors and clippers.

Without Leo around to soak up the overabundance of feelings, she was going to burn out. She sighed. They should talk. Probably. Maybe. He'd left without confirming it yesterday. Not much more she could do or say, although God, she wanted to.

Damn, those darn tears again. Ducking her head to pretend she had more to pack, she made a quick swipe of her face, hoping no one saw. That was a conversation she could do without.

She just wanted to go home and let go of her control in private.

"Thanks so much for today," Jovy said, walking toward them. "You both made a lot of people happy."

They decided to hold the clinic in the rec room at the house because it was familiar to some and had a friendly, relaxed vibe. Group therapy was held there, plus the pool table gave the ones waiting something to do.

Fi smiled and waved a hand. "Ah. We were happy to. This was a great idea."

Kaydee decided to let those two talk. She wasn't much in the mood anyhow. Kind of all talked out from the conversations with those she'd worked on, and the fussing and gushing from the women about the baby when she'd first arrived.

Shock had hit her first, followed by hope—that mean bitch. It'd resurfaced to flutter in her chest, making her think things might actually be okay. Why would Leo tell them about the baby if he wasn't happy?

Then reality had set in and snuffed hope out cold. If he was happy he would've come back last night. Or called. Or come over this morning or made a damn effort to seek her out. She was on his ranch, for God's sake.

No. It'd probably just slipped out of his mouth like it had slipped out of hers yesterday.

Inhaling, she snapped her case shut and stood. "Well, I'm ready if you are, Fi," she said, hoping her friend picked up on her "get me the hell out of here" vibe.

Fi had insisted on driving today, and Kaydee let her, happy to close her eyes and take a nap on the way down. Exactly what she planned to do on the way home. At least her crazy fatigue was handy for something.

Fi exchanged a look with Jovy before she met her gaze. "Sure."

Kaydee was too tired to wonder what that was all about. She'd worry later. Right now, she was ready to go.

"Don't forget this," Jovy said, handing Fiona the donation jar that they tried all day to convince the woman they didn't want. It fell on deaf ears. Stone had warned them his wife was stubborn. "And you don't need to leave yet," Jovy said. "Why don't you stay for some cake or Vince's cannoli? They really are to die for. And there's a delivery coming later you're going to want to see. Trust me."

As tempting as all that sounded, especially the cannoli part, Kaydee shook her head. "No thanks." She glanced sideways at Jovy as they walked to the front door. "I'm kind of beat, sorry. Maybe next time."

If she thought sticking around to see Leo would help, she would, but she was a realist. It was best to leave. He needed to come to his own conclusion about them. No sense in trying to tip the scale her way.

"Of course." The woman stopped as they reached the front door. "Speaking of next time, are you both good with keeping the clinic on the last Sunday of every month?

She glanced at Fi, who nodded. "That works."

Coming here every month was going to kill her if Leo decided he didn't want to be a part of her life…or the baby's, but she'd do it for the veterans. And maybe Leo would remain scarce like today, although his absence didn't alleviate the ache pressing against her chest.

Was it always going to feel like that?

Kaydee blinked back her stupid tears again, opened the door, and gasped.

Leo…

Looking exactly how she loved—badass and sexy—he stood on the porch, leaning against a post, with a dozen roses in one hand, a bag in the other, and a look in his eyes that said she was the most important thing in the world to him.

Fi removed the case from Kaydee's hand and said something, but Kaydee didn't catch it. Her heart was smashing into her ribs with swift, erratic beats that thundered in her ears.

He's here. Actually here.

But her brain wasn't, because she couldn't seem to remember how to move. She kind of just stood there and blinked at him and his Ranger buddies standing in the driveway behind him. They had his back. That thought managed to flash through her mind, and she blinked again. Dammit.

"I'm so sorry, Kaydee," Leo said, his tone deep and warm with emotion as he stepped toward her. "Sorry for being an ass," he said. "I shouldn't have walked away from you yesterday. Shouldn't have let you think you don't matter to me, because you do. So damn much. If you can find it in you to give me another chance, I swear I'll never leave you again."

A familiar sensation returned to swarm her chest. Hope. Kaydee fought an inner battle on whether to allow it to blossom or die. Did she dare take another chance? Did she dare believe him?

Leo stopped in front of her and offered two red roses. "I hope you can forgive me," he said, but before she could find her voice and reply, he handed her two more. "These are for believing in me...even though I didn't and was a stupid ass."

She choked out a half laugh, half sob.

"Damn straight," Brick said, and the crowd chuckled.

Two more roses made it into her grasp. "These are for being the sweet, caring woman I don't deserve. And these are for wanting me anyway," he said, handing her two more.

By now, her hands were shaking, and she had to keep blinking and swallowing to fight the burning in her eyes and throat.

"Oh, that was a good one," Fi muttered while Jovy sighed

dreamily behind her.

"I wish you could see yourself the way I do," he said. "The way you donate your time to others. Sacrifice for your family. Step out of your comfort zone so a couple of amorous octogenarians can have an all-nighter."

"Thank you, honey," Ava said.

Kaydee blinked and focused on his grandmother standing next to her smiling grandfather in the crowd. Her heart swelled, and she met Leo's smiling gaze. "You fetched them?"

"Yes." His smile broadened. "It wouldn't be right to profess my love for you without them here."

Love?

Her grip on emotions slipped, and hope exploded to life inside her, interfering with her ability to draw a breath. "You love me?" she whispered.

"God, yeah, I love you." His voice was low but fierce as he handed her two more roses. "That's what these are for. Because I love you. I love everything about you. The way you put yourself out there for me, even though it means straying into uncharted territory. The way you look at me. God, I love that. And the way you saved me."

She frowned. "You didn't need saving, Leo."

He'd done that all on his own. He was the one who'd turned it all around. Found the courage to ask for help. Made himself happy. And she was so damn proud of him for doing that.

"Yes, I *did* need saving," he said. "From myself. You made me realize that *I* wasn't toxic. Holding on to my past was."

Oh God…he got it. He finally got it.

And she wanted to get closer to him. To touch him. But she could tell by the determined gleam in his eyes he had things he needed to say, so she remained still, silently willing him to continue.

"I like this present me. I like who I am with you," he

said. "And I want to be the man *you* want to step out of your comfort zone with."

She smiled. "You are. You so are."

He answered with a grin. "I want to be the man you want to spend the rest of your life with."

Air backed up in her throat, and she cleared it as he handed her the last four roses, his gaze fierce, protective, and warm. So warm. "These are for carrying my baby and wanting me—I hope—to share your lives. My world doesn't work without you in it, Kaydee. I don't like the me without you."

Her heart squeezed, and her eyes filled again. It was too much. Perfect. Right. She was done. That was it. She needed to hold him. Touch him. Love him. She was shaking so bad her teeth were practically chattering, and the poor roses were rustling so hard it was a wonder the petals didn't fall off.

"Give me them," Fi said, sticking her hand around Kaydee, as if reading her mind.

She handed off the flowers, then turned back to Leo.

"Hang on," Beth said, rushing forward to tug the bag and chocolates from Leo before scurrying back to stand by her husband in the crowd. "Carry on."

She smiled her thanks to the woman before returning her attention to Leo. "I'll let you in on a secret," she said, stepping closer to touch his face. "I recently discovered I don't like the me I am without you, either. She's too closed up. Miserable."

He reached out to place his hands on her hips. "I can help with that."

She chuckled. "I know. I also know another secret. I love you, too, Leo. So much I think my heart might burst."

Joy brightened his gaze, and soon it blazed. She knew that look. He was going to kiss her. Her nearly bursting heart leaped. And when he hauled her in close and their lips met, her entire body came alive. She was acutely aware of all of him, right down to the way he held her tight like he would never let her go. She really, really loved that part.

When he finally broke the kiss, she barely heard the crowd's applause, for she was hyperaware that a certain body part of his—her favorite part of his—was hyperaware of her, too.

A smile tugged her lips. "You really are happy to see me."

He choked out a laugh and leaned in for another quick kiss. "With every breath."

"Okay, I've got to know," Fiona spoke up from behind. "What's in the bag?"

She felt another laugh vibrate from him before he drew back and turned to Beth. The woman grinned and scooted forward to hand the bag back.

"Brick needs to take some pointers," Beth whispered loudly with a wink before retreating back to her frowning husband.

"Hey," Brick said.

She glanced from the red bag Leo placed in her hand up to his still-smiling face. "What is it?"

Leo shrugged, his gaze alight with mischief. "Something I thought you'd like our baby to have."

Our baby...

Tears sprang to her eyes, and this time she let them spill out. God, it felt so good to hear him say that. She blinked a few times as she dug in the bag to pull out a small, stuffed... "Captain America?"

"Good choice," Emma said.

Leo smiled. "Figured it didn't matter, boy or girl, everyone loves Cap."

Nodding, she drew in a breath. "And I love you." She lifted up to kiss his cheek. "And my surprises. I just feel bad I don't have anything for you."

"No need," he said, gently holding her face in his hands while he wiped her wet cheeks with his thumbs. "*You* are my greatest surprise."

Epilogue

It was a typical Sunday in May, and Leo was kicking back with his buddies on the ranch porch, watching their wives playing some kind of humorous card game at a picnic table under the large oak. Big cow lying at Stone's feet, her ears twitching every time the wind carried the women's laughter up to them.

Leo could easily pick out Kaydee's sweet tone. It never failed to trip his heart.

Neither did she.

"When we left active duty, did any of you ever think we'd be doing this?" Stone asked, looking out over the Texas landscape, beer in one hand while petting the cow with the other.

Brick glanced at his beer. "Drinking?"

"Shooting the shit?" Leo asked.

Cord raised a brow. "Sitting on the porch?"

Vince chuckled. "Petting your pet cow?"

"No, you assholes," Stone groused.

"Watching our wives play cards?" Vince tried again with a grin.

"That, for one." Stone pointed to Vince. "Who would've ever thought we'd all be married and settled someday?"

"Or that Leo and Stone would be dads soon." Vince grinned before taking a pull of his beer.

"Leo? Sure," Brick said. "But my brother? No way." The goof shook his head, but Leo saw the mock surprise on his face.

Stone frowned. "Why wouldn't you think I could be a dad?"

"Because you're a mother hen, not a father hen." Brick snickered, then laughed outright when his brother flipped him off.

Leo laughed along with his buddies, and his heart lifted as he watched Kaydee leave the game and approach with a hand on her back and the most adorable waddle. Jovy wasn't far behind.

"Duty calls," Stone said with a grin, then glanced at the cow. "That means you behave, Lula Belle."

The cow mooed.

Unlike Kaydee, who was due any day, Jovy still had a few months. But Leo knew those backaches didn't care how much time you had left. Or if it was the middle of night or day.

"Hey." Kaydee gave him a quick peck on the cheek. "Need your magical hands."

Brick grimaced. "TMI."

Cord whacked the idiot so Leo didn't have to.

"Sure." He motioned for her to turn around, then he helped her sit on his lap and got to work applying pressure low on her spine, smiling at her moans and how uncomfortable it made Brick.

"Me, too, hun," Jovy said to Stone, then death-glared the

cow before settling on her husband's lap for the same.

"How was the game?" Leo asked Kaydee.

She shrugged, too busy pressing into his hand and sighing. At that moment, he was pretty sure he was the luckiest bastard in the world. And it made him revisit Stone's earlier question and revise it a little.

If someone had told Leo last year that this spring he'd be happily married, expecting a baby any day now, a Foxtrot supervisor, and part owner of At-Ease, he would've laughed in their face and asked what they were smoking.

Not necessarily in that order.

But here he was, sitting on the porch at the ranch, rubbing the back of his very beautiful, very pregnant wife while she sat on his leg…at least it looked like she sat on his leg. Hard to tell since he'd started to lose feeling a minute ago.

"So, you two heading home today or staying another night?" Stone asked, hand on Jovy's spine, using the other to keep Lula Belle's tail from hitting his wife.

It was weird how the cow's tail suddenly started to wag—excessively—once Jovy had arrived.

"We're heading back today," he said.

Until her dad retired in a little over a year and her parents moved to Texas, Kaydee and Leo had decided to live in Dallas to be close to her grandfather. It meant an hour commute each way for him, but he didn't care. It was worth it to come home to a happy wife.

He'd proposed not long after he'd moved in with her, and three months ago, they said their I dos right here on the ranch, just like all his buddies before him.

"How's your grandmother and Nate?" Vince sat back in his chair and grinned. "They're my heroes, deejaying at the rec center."

Kaydee grunted. "Until music blares through the walls at two a.m. because they're 'mixing.' I told them that was so not happening when the baby's here."

"For sure," Jovy said, then her face brightened as a large truck rumbled to a stop in the driveway. "Oh, good. He's here." She clapped her hands, glee claiming her expression. Her discomfort was apparently forgotten as she stood and walked around Lula Belle without batting an eye.

That was new. No Lula Belle barbs or death glares.

"He? He, who?" Stone frowned, rushing after his wife as she practically skipped to the truck...which wasn't easy to do considering her baby belly.

Kaydee rose to her feet, and Leo silently gave thanks as he rose, too, shaking out his numb leg, urging the blood flow.

Leo glanced at Kaydee. "Do you know about this?"

"No." She shook her head and patted her swollen belly. "All I know are bathrooms at this point. And that you give the best back rubs."

He moved behind her to dip his head and brush his mouth to her ear. "That's not all I'm good at rubbing," he whispered.

She laughed and set her head to his chest. "I remember those days."

He snorted. "You forgot last night?"

She'd enjoyed herself last night. He knew it. So did the neighbors.

"Jovy, what did you do?" Stone's shocked tone brought Leo's mind back to the present and he watched as the truck drove off, leaving a smiling Jovy and a very big brown-and-white cow in the driveway.

"What does it look like?" She snorted.

Or was that the cow?

"I bought Lula Belle a boyfriend." A smug smile curved the woman's lips. "Let's go, Raging Moo. Get up. It's time to meet Bucky."

Kaydee laughed. "Great name." Amusement lit her eyes as she smiled at him.

He groaned, far less amused.

Seriously? Would he ever get away from the Marvel references?

"Could've been worse." Brick snickered. "Could've been Sebastian."

"Or Stan." Vince grinned.

He mentally flipped them both off. Cord, Vince, and Brick laughed, and Bucky turned toward the sound, and watched as Stone managed to coax Lula Belle to her feet. She stretched, then slowly made her way to the driveway.

"Yes!" Jovy smiled, patting Bucky's back. "Here she comes, boy. Go get her."

Kaydee inhaled. "He's actually doing it."

Leo shook his head, wondering if anyone from their old unit would believe him if he told them about this. Holding back a snicker, he watched as the two cows moseyed closer and sniffed each other. Everything looked promising, until they mooed, and Lula Belle turned and walked back to Stone.

"No." Jovy frowned. "No…that's not what's supposed to happen."

Brick and Vince laughed, followed by Cord.

Bucky's head jerked at the sound.

"What the hell was that?" Cord asked, brows crashing together, glancing from Jovy to Stone to Bucky…who mooed at him.

Jovy scratched her forehead. "I don't understand. That should've worked. Maybe we did it wrong. There's got to be something I missed."

"Think faster," Cord said, his gaze narrowing as the cow began to trot his way. "Jovy?"

"It's not my fault!" she said, wringing her hands. "Are all the damn cows in Texas defective?"

Kaydee leaned against Leo and laughed. "This is better than Netflix."

"Stone. Dammit. Do something," Cord said, his tone more insistent than Leo had ever heard. Hell, the guy had faced down insurgents without batting an eye. "He's not stopping."

"Use your Warlock stare," Brick suggested with a laugh.

Leo knew he shouldn't, but he laughed, too. He couldn't help it. It was damn funny.

"Lula Belle." Jovy marched over to the cow grazing near Stone's feet. "What did you say to Bucky? You broke him."

The cow stopped grazing, raised her head, looked at Jovy, then mooed. Bucky didn't react, unless you counted sniffing Cord's crotch.

Cord reacted, though. He cursed and hopped up onto the porch. Apparently only Lula Belle knew how to climb steps, because Bucky stayed in the yard, but paced the length of the porch. "Jesus," Cord grumbled. "Could this day get any crazier?"

Kaydee cleared her throat. "Uh, does my water breaking count?"

Leo's heart slammed into his throat. He jerked his head in her direction and blinked. "Seriously?"

She nodded. "Yes."

Damn. Their doctor and hospital were in Dallas—over an hour away. "Are you okay?" He grabbed her hand, and it shook, so he brought it to his chest…and that's when he realized he was the one shaking.

"I'm fine." She smiled, a calm, beautiful smile that immediately grounded him.

He leaned in to brush his lips to her forehead. "I love you."

"I love you, too," she said, squeezing his hand.

"What do we do?" Brick's panic tone startled the cows. "Should I boil water?"

Vince snorted. "Yeah, sure. If we were in the movies."

Leo glanced at the faces now crowded around them. "Okay. Looks like we're having a baby." He gave out orders. It never even dawned on him to panic. A far cry from the man he was when he'd first set foot on the ranch three years ago.

Leo and Cord helped Kaydee settle into the back seat of Kaydee's car that Jovy had covered with a few towels. Thank God they hadn't come down to Joyful in his truck. He climbed in the back with her because Cord insisted on driving them, and because his buddy was an army medic, Leo didn't argue, just in case their baby decided to arrive super quick.

As it turned out, their little girl was very considerate, not only waiting until they got to the hospital, she waited for their doctor to arrive, and all their family and friends—except for Kaydee's parents, who were catching the first flight in the morning.

Watching his wife cradle their little girl, something inside Leo clicked into place. He hadn't realized anything was out of place. Being with Kaydee made him whole. Now he was... solid.

"How do you feel?" he asked, brushing his wife's temple with his lips.

"Happy," she said, her tone hoarse with emotion. "So happy." She glanced up at him. "You?"

"Complete," he said firmly.

Kaydee's eyes filled with tears, which spilled down her face as she handed their daughter to him.

Their daughter...

A fierce rush of emotion washed through him as he held the tiny little miracle. The second-best surprise of his life. He dipped down to gently brush his lips to her temple, like he had her mom.

There was a time in his life when he hated surprises. They brought death and pain and filled him with so much agony the very act of breathing hurt. But then Kaydee showed him that life held good surprises, too. Ones that filled his heart with so much joy and happiness that losing his breath could be a great thing.

"Have you decided on a name?" he asked quietly, never taking his eyes off the sweet, innocent angel. She had her mother's cute little upturned nose, brown hair, and his blue eyes.

"Yes," Kaydee said. "There's only one name that's fitting to me. One name that's perfect. I knew it when I carried her. And I knew it was even more fitting the second I saw her."

He smiled down at his baby girl, who already had him wrapped around her little finger. "What is it?"

"Hope."

And just like that, *hope* burned away the last of the shadows hiding behind his heart. "Perfect."

Acknowledgments

A super huge thank you to my editor Heather Howland for all your help, and time, and insight, not only on this book, but on the entire Men of At-Ease Ranch series. This book was very special, and I'm so happy we were able to give Leo his HEA!

Entangled, and the Lovestruck team, is always a joy to work with. Thank you for all you do!

Once again, I'd like to acknowledge my husband and thank him for his military knowledge. Love you!

To pumpkin spice creamer for flavoring my many, many mugs of coffee.

And to the cats for bringing lots of comic relief and companionship during some long hours. Love you all!

And, as always, to you, the readers, thank you for continuing to pick up my books and for taking the time to email me with kind words and your wonderful reviews.

About the Author

Donna Michaels is an award-winning, *New York Times* and *USA Today* bestselling author of Romaginative fiction. Her hot, humorous, and heartwarming stories include cowboys, men in uniform, and some sexy primal alphas who are equally matched by their heroines. With a husband recently retired from the military, a household of seven, and several rescued cats, she never runs out of material to write, and has rightfully earned the nickname Lucy...and sometimes Ethel. From short to epic, her books entertain readers across a variety of subgenres, and one was even hand-drawn into a Japanese translation. Now, if only she could read it.

To learn more about Donna Michaels and her books, or to join her mailing list, visit www.DonnaMichaelsAuthor.com.

Find love in unexpected places with these Lovestrucks...

HER SUPER-SECRET REBOUND BOYFRIEND
a novel by Kerri Carpenter

It wasn't shy librarian Lola McBride's idea to crash someone else's high school reunion. Her best friend made her do it, insisting that having fun with a super-hot rebound would make her forget about her breakup. That's when she meets the hottest guy she's ever seen. Architect Luke Erickson catches the sexy brunette in a lie, and counters with a proposal. From one reunion to another, Lola and Luke are suddenly spending a lot of time together. Good thing they're only pretending, or this super-secret relationship could get really complicated.

THREE DAY FIANCEE
an *Animal Attraction* novel by Marissa Clarke

Between helicopter pilot Taylor Blankenship's job, his dog, and his matchmaking grandmother, he has no time for anyone or anything—especially a woman. The job of New York City dog walker suits Caitlin Ramos perfectly while she preps for her CPA exam. Men suck. Especially her bossy, hot client with the Saint Bernard that thinks it's a lap dog. Offered a bargain she can't refuse, Caitlin finds herself playing the part of fiancée to Taylor. All she has to do is fake a relationship with Mr. Bossy Pants in front of his entire family and not lose her heart to a guy who turns out to be a lot more than she'd bargained for.

DRIVEN TO TEMPTATION
a *Driven to Love* novel by Melia Alexander

Aidan Ross might be an engineering genius, but people skills? Not this soldier's forte. Thankfully, a trusted friend is accompanying him to a make-or-break tradeshow...but then a bubbly redhead hops into his truck, claiming to be his new road trip buddy. She's a gorgeous distraction he can't afford. Or ignore.

Made in the USA
Monee, IL
09 January 2025

76415137R00125